The BARN at GUN LAKE

The Gun Lake Gang Adventure Series
BOOK 1

Johnnie Tuitel and Sharon Lamson

CEDAR TREE PUBLISHING

Clovis, California

THE BARN AT GUN LAKE
Copyright 1998 by Johnnie Tuitel and Sharon E. Lamson

Published by  Cedar Tree Publishing
2455 Norcrest Drive
Muskegon, MI 49441
1-888-302-7463 (toll free)

Cover, Book Design and Illustration: Eduardo Pilande

Library of Congress Catalog-in-Publication Data
Lamson, Sharon E., 1948—
Tuitel, Johnnie, 1963—
The Barn at Gun Lake/Johnnie Tuitel and Sharon Lamson

p.   cm.—(The Gun Lake Adventure Series)
Summary: Johnnie, who has cerebral palsy and is in a wheelchair, finds himself with two challenges: gaining acceptance from his newfound friends and solving an unusual pirating mystery.
ISBN 0-9658075-0-9

[1. Adventure stories—Fiction   2. Mystery and detective stories—Fiction 3. Physically Handicapped—Children—Fiction
4. Michigan—Fiction]

I. Title   II. Series: Lamson, Sharon E., 1948—, Tuitel, Johnnie, 1963—
(The Gun Lake Gang Adventure Series)

97-066781

Dedication

To my parents who believed in me and encouraged me to not just live, but to thrive. And to my wife Debbie who lovingly taught me that it is OK to be me.

—*JOHNNIE TUITEL*

To my husband Robert whose belief in and encouragement of me have been both humbling and motivating. And to my youngest daughter Robyn who introduced me to Johnnie Tuitel.

—*SHARON E. LAMSON*

TABLE OF CONTENTS

CHAPTER ONE

The Initiation

JOHNNIE JACOBSON'S HANDS GRIPPED THE HANDRIMS OF his wheelchair so tightly, his knuckles turned white. Pushing his chair down a dirt driveway was no easy job. He could have used his crutches, but he thought wheeling would be easier. Now he wasn't so sure.

Johnnie, who was born with cerebral palsy, had good upper body strength. He could "walk" with the help of crutches, though it made him tired. Unlike people with more severe cerebral palsy, or CP as he called it, he could speak clearly with only a slight slur. People usually commented on his bright smile and cheerful attitude. His parents and sisters also knew that behind those dark brown eyes was a lot of mischief.

Often kids asked Johnnie what CP was. He'd answer by saying: "You know what a computer is, right? What happens if you want to type the word 'cat' and have it appear on your computer's monitor? Well, you'd begin by pressing the letter 'c' on the keyboard. A signal from the computer would tell the word processor to place that letter on the screen.

"Our brain is like a computer. When I want to scratch my nose, for example, my brain sends a signal to my finger and tells it to scratch my nose.

"In my case, my personal brain computer became partly broken. When I was born three months too early, I was placed in a incubator. In there I was kept warm and fed oxygen so I could survive. Unfortunately, I was given too much oxygen, and it damaged part of my brain. The affected parts of my brain don't send the right signals to certain parts of my body—in my case my legs and part of my speech center."

This explanation usually satisfied kids' curiosity. And when his friends saw all that he could do, they soon forgot about Johnnie's disability.

A lot of Johnnie's positive attitude was a result of having a loving family. From the time Johnnie was little, his mother and father encouraged him to try new things. They never did for him what they knew he could do for himself. He learned how to ride a tricycle, swim, dive and play sports. Johnnie grew up believing there wasn't anything he couldn't do if he put his mind to it.

And right now Johnnie knew he had to put his mind to getting to that barn. Johnnie looked at the long, winding driveway, took a deep breath and nudged the wheels of his chair forward. As he trudged along, he was aware that his newfound friends were watching him. It was part of the initiation.

At one point, when he hit a rut in the road and had a hard time pushing past it, he muttered, "If it weren't for that kid—what's his name? Oh, yeah, Travis Hughes—the one with the big mouth—one of the other kids would have pushed me down to the barn. But, no! Travis Rogers didn't want me in the neighborhood club to begin with. He said, 'We don't want anyone in the Gun Lake Gang who can't hold his own.'"

Indeed, Travis had looked disgusted when the other kids had invited Johnnie to join. Travis, who was 11 years old, the same age and grade as Johnnie, was considered to be the school's best athlete. He was tall and built like a junior football player—which he was. In the summer his sandy brown hair bleached out almost white in the sun, and his tanned skin brought out the blue in his eyes. Complete with dimples, he was a guy the girls didn't mind looking at. Travis was a good student too. In fact, he was a member of the student government at his middle school. He was a kid used to being a leader and used to getting his own way.

Though he was popular, Travis didn't have much time for other kids who didn't "measure up" to his standards.

So when Johnnie Jacobson moved into the neighborhood, Travis took one look at the leg braces, crutches and then the wheelchair and decided Johnnie was a "loser." It was only after the other kids in the club insisted on giving Johnnie a chance that Travis agreed to let him go through the initiation.

Johnnie had accepted the challenge with an "I'll-show-you" attitude. But now, here he was about halfway down the long, winding driveway heading toward the old abandoned barn, thinking that this initiation was more like "mission impossible." According to the rules of the initiation, he had to go into the barn and retrieve something to prove he had gone inside. Then and only then would he be allowed to become a member of the Gun Lake Gang.

The sun was getting low in the summer sky. Luckily in West Michigan, the summer evenings were long. Johnnie thought about the move he and his family had made from California to Michigan only a few weeks ago. Getting used to all the towering trees, the sandy soil and the cooler air was difficult. But looking out at Lake Michigan reminded Johnnie of the Pacific Ocean. At first Johnnie couldn't believe that a lake could be so big and have currents and waves. True, the tides weren't as noticeable as the ocean's tides and the waves weren't as big, but to Johnnie, Lake Michigan was a friendly reminder of "home."

Breathing a little harder, Johnnie forced his mind away from the lake and back to the job he had to do. After much pushing and grunting, Johnnie made his way to the old barn. He took time to quickly push away a strand of his dark-brown hair from his eyes as he looked at the big building in front of him.

The barn stood weather-worn and in need of repair. It was a typical barn with huge doors and a hayloft window up toward where the roof formed a peak. Though most of the original paint had peeled or faded away, Johnnie could tell that at one time the barn had been painted red. His friends told him that a Mr. McGruther had lived in the farmhouse that once stood near the shore of Gun Lake, not too far from where the barn was. After his young wife died suddenly, Mr. McGruther stayed pretty much to himself. When he died at the age of 86, some thirty years ago, the land was given to a distant relative, according to the instructions in Mr. McGruther's will. But no one ever claimed it and so the house and the barn remained empty.

Then about five years ago a severe thunderstorm blew in off the lake and the house was struck by lightning. It had pretty much burned to the ground before the fire department could put out the blaze. Now, only the barn remained.

It rested on a cleared area of land. Just 50 yards away from the barn, towering oaks, maples, birch and sassafras trees formed a thick green canopy in the spring and summer months. Rambling wild blackberry bushes grew everywhere and were laden with sweet berries. Getting to them was difficult, however, because of their thorny branches. Gray, red and black squirrels scurried along the ground and climbed the giant trees effortlessly. Deer, raccoons, possums, skunks, foxes, moles and rabbits made their homes along the ground or in the trees, while many kinds of birds flew overhead.

A narrow footpath led through the woods and out onto the giant sand dune, which sloped sharply down to the sandy shores of Gun Lake. Once out on the dune, sea gulls could be seen circling gracefully over the water looking for fish.

Like many of the small lakes in West Michigan, Gun Lake was connected to Lake Michigan through a narrow channel. Mr. McGruther had owned most of the land around Gun Lake, and so there were no other homesites. The lake was surrounded on three sides by huge sand dunes. Just about the only thing growing on the sandy slopes were clumps of long, broad-leafed dune grass that bent and swayed in the wind. Most of the beach was smooth, but there were parts where huge boulders jutted out into the water from the shore, making traveling around Gun Lake by foot very difficult.

Johnnie hardly noticed his surroundings. He was intent on getting into the barn, finding something and leaving. "No fair just getting hay," Travis had insisted.

Johnnie was tired from pushing his wheelchair. The long shadows stretching across the road encouraged his mind to remember all the ghost stories he had ever heard. With renewed determination, he gave his wheelchair a few more pushes toward the barn doors—only to discover they were locked.

Though he was tempted to give up, Travis' sharp words prodded him to find some way of getting inside. The other kids must have done it, he thought.

Johnnie inched along the side of the barn looking for loose boards or another door. As he rounded the corner to the back of the barn, his search was rewarded. Another set of barn doors greeted him—and they weren't nailed shut. However, a padlock secured a chain that was looped through the door handles. Frustrated, Johnnie grabbed the padlock, gritted his teeth and yanked on it. To his surprise, the lock gave way. He quickly pulled the lock out of the chain and threw it to the ground. Then slowly, he opened the barn doors. The fading rays of the setting sun illuminated the entrance, making it easy for Johnnie to look inside.

The barn looked empty with only a smattering of hay on the ground. *What am I supposed to take back—dirt?* Johnnie wondered to himself. He opened the doors wide to let in as much sunlight as he could. Carefully he wheeled inside. Soon, Johnnie's eyes grew accustomed to the dimness. High above him hung some old tools, but he knew he'd never be able to reach them. He saw several stalls where farm animals had once stayed. As he moved toward one of the stalls, something shiny caught his eye. Johnnie pushed his wheelchair toward the object and was surprised to find a square piece of plastic. Upon closer examination Johnnie could tell that it was the plastic cover to a compact disc—a CD.

Johnnie picked up the cover, opened it and noticed it was empty. He put it beside him in his seat. "Hmmm," Johnnie said aloud, "I wonder what a CD is doing in a place like this? Maybe some kids had a party down here!"

Just then his eye caught sight of what appeared to be a door. It was constructed in such a way that it actually looked like part of the wall. There was no door handle, just a small hole in the wood. Because the hinges were on the inside, the door swung in instead of out.

"Wow! A secret room!" Johnnie exclaimed. The opening of the doorway was narrow, and Johnnie knew he wouldn't be able to fit his chair inside. He opened the door and looked inside. The only light filtering into the room came through the cracks in the outside walls. Johnnie squinted his eyes, trying hard to see. Though he couldn't tell for sure, it seemed to him that there were stacks of boxes piled on both sides of the room with just a narrow pathway between.

Johnnie could have scooted out of his wheelchair and used his arms to pull himself across the dirt floor, but the idea of being in a dark, strange place without his wheelchair gave Johnnie second thoughts. As he fingered the plastic CD cover next to him, he decided that he'd better get out of there.

He backed up his wheelchair and put his finger in the hole in the door to pull it shut. Then he turned around and headed toward the open door.

Once out into the fresh late-evening air, he breathed a sigh of relief. He pushed the barn doors shut and looked around for the padlock. It was simply too dim to see much of anything on the ground. He found the chain and put it back through the door handles. "At least that will keep the doors shut," he said to himself. He figured the padlock would just have to remain on the ground. Maybe tomorrow some of the kids could come and put it back through the chain.

For now, Johnnie's only thoughts were wheeling his

way back up the long driveway. He hoped that his friends had waited for him. Suddenly he heard a rustling in the woods to his left. Robyn Anderson, one of his new friends, ran up to his chair.

"There you are!" she said, her voice filled with concern. "It's getting dark and some of us had to go home. I told the others that I would wait, but then I thought I'd better come looking for you."

"Thanks! But I'm OK," Johnnie said. Inside he was genuinely glad to see Robyn. She was almost 11 years old and attended Gun Lake Middle School, just as Johnnie would in the fall. She was tall and thin, and if Johnnie didn't know better, Robyn could easily pass for a boy. Her short brown hair was sun-bleached on the top and was cut above her ears. Robyn, who enjoyed rollerblading, soccer and bike riding, wasn't into jewelry or makeup. She was competitive in just about everything she did—sports, school and games of any kind. Robyn had been one of the first neighborhood kids to come over to Johnnie's new house the day he and his family moved in. And she had been one of the kids who had argued with Travis to let Johnnie into their club.

"Need any help wheeling back up this driveway?" Robyn asked.

Johnnie considered saying no, but then something his Dutch grandmother used to say came back to him. She'd always tell him, "Pride goeth before destruction and a haughty heart before a fall." He smiled up at Robyn who was waiting for an answer. "Yeah, I sure could use some help. This driveway was a lot longer than I thought it was."

Then he pulled up the CD case and said, "Hey, Robyn. Look at what I found in the barn. Do you think some teenagers are having parties down there?"

Robyn took the CD from Johnnie's outstretched hand. "Parties? Down there?" she said, scrunching up her face. "Nah! There's no electricity down there. How would they play CDs?"

CHAPTER TWO

CD Pirates

WARM RAYS OF SUNLIGHT SLOWLY CREPT between the slats of Johnnie's closed mini-blinds. The lighted room and smell of fresh morning air gently awakened him. Johnnie turned over to look at his clock. "Hmm, it's only seven o'clock," he said sleepily. "I think I'll just roll over and close my eyes a few minutes longer."

He was about to drift off to sleep when the statement that Robyn had made the night before, about there being no electricity down at the barn, jolted Johnnie awake. "The CD!" he gasped. He sat up and grabbed his clothes that were laid out on the chair next to his bed. This was going to be the day he showed the rest of the kids what he had found in the barn. Johnnie felt a tingle of excitement go down his spine as he anticipated the unfolding mystery about where the CD had come from and what it was doing in McGruther's barn.

Johnnie slid into his wheelchair, opened the door to his bedroom and wheeled across the hall to the bathroom. While combing his hair and washing his face, Johnnie could not stop thinking about what the other kids would say when he showed them what he had found. "Even Travis will have to admit I can hold my own," Johnnie said to his reflection in the mirror. "After all, I did make it down to the barn by myself, and I found something inside—just like the initiation rules said."

Johnnie pushed himself down the hallway and turned left into the dining room. From the dining room Johnnie turned right into the kitchen where his mother was fixing breakfast. His dad was already seated at the kitchen table reading the morning newspaper. He lowered the paper as Johnnie came in. "Good morning!" he said. "You're up early this morning!"

"Yeah! My friends and I are going to the schoolyard later this morning."

"So, things are going OK for you?" his mother asked as she placed a bowl of cereal and some juice on the table for her son. "You seem to have made quite a few friends already!"

"They're really nice," Johnnie said as he poured milk on his cereal. "They've even let me into their club!"

"What kind of a club is this?" Johnnie's dad asked as he sipped his coffee.

"You know—a club!" Johnnie answered. "It's just a bunch of kids from school—well, and Danny's little sister Katy and Joey Thomas, who go to the elementary school. We have club meetings and do—you know—stuff."

"I did meet that little girl Robyn Anderson yesterday," said Johnnie's mom. "She seemed very friendly. And I would like to meet the other kids too. Why don't we see if they can come over for lunch this afternoon?"

Johnnie thought about it for a moment. He knew his parents trusted him and that they wanted him to fit in, and he also knew they would want to meet his friends before they let him go off to play away from home for hours at a time. He had come home a little late last night, and his parents had worried. In fact, his dad was out with a flashlight looking for him. He guessed it was only fair that his parents meet his friends. Besides, he was proud of his family.

Johnnie's grandparents (both his mother's parents and his father's) had immigrated to the United States from the Netherlands during World War II. They had been among many Dutch people who had fled from Hitler's army. Both Johnnie's mother and father had been born in Grand Rapids, Michigan, after the war had ended. They met in high school and fell in love. After high school, Johnnie's father wanted to attend a maritime academy and follow in the footsteps of his Dutch ancestors who were in the Merchant Marine. He applied and was accepted at the maritime academy in Vallejo, California. This, of course, meant that he and his young bride would have to leave Michigan to attend the four-year school. After he graduated, he and his wife stayed in California and Johnnie's dad landed a job aboard an oil freighter.

Soon after, Johnnie's older sisters and brother were born and then came Johnnie—the baby of the family. When Johnnie was about 18 months old, the Jacobsons noticed their son wasn't doing all the things his older sisters and brother had done at that age. Worried, they took him to the doctor who conducted several types of medical tests on him.

Test results in hand, the doctor told the Jacobsons their son had cerebral palsy. "He won't talk. He won't walk. He won't be able to go to school. I think you should just put him away in a special institution where professionals can care for him," he said bluntly.

But Johnnie's parents had different thoughts. They loved their son, and they weren't about to give up on him. Both of his parents believed in Johnnie and trusted in God to help him. As he grew, they helped him ride a tricycle when he was little. They encouraged him to try everything he wanted to try. He could walk a little with crutches, but it was slow and so Johnnie used a wheelchair to get around. As he grew, Johnnie developed in many ways, like most children do. He could talk and was a good student at school. Obviously, the doctor had been wrong about Johnnie.

Johnnie and his family loved California. But when oil prices rose and the demand for oil dropped, Johnnie's father found himself out of a job. For awhile, he tried to find work in California.

One day Johnnie's grandfather called and told the family about an engineering job with one of the boat-building companies along Michigan's west shoreline. The job called for an engineer who would help design and build yachts and sailing vessels used mostly for recreation. This work would be somewhat different than the one Mr. Jacobson had in California, but the family agreed the job would be a good one. Plus moving back to Michigan and being close to family again sounded great.

Soon after Johnnie's eleventh birthday, the Jacobsons moved back to Michigan. Though Johnnie hated to say good-bye to his friends and teachers, he was excited to live closer to his grandparents. He had been to Michigan only twice in his whole life—once when he was one year old and another time when he was five.

Though he was excited, he worried that the kids in Michigan wouldn't accept him with his disability. He knew people would look at him and ask questions. That was OK with Johnnie, but he didn't like it when people were rude, disrespectful and said mean things.

In fact, Johnnie was pleasantly surprised to find that most of the kids in his new neighborhood were friendly and adventuresome. His only "challenge" so far was Travis. While Travis hadn't said any mean things, he had made it clear that he didn't think Johnnie could "keep up" with the rest of them.

Johnnie glanced at the clock. It was 8:00 AM. I wonder if it's too early to call Robyn, he wondered. Just then the telephone rang.

"Johnnie, it's for you," his mother said as she handed him the telephone receiver.

"Hello!" Johnnie said.

"Hi!" came Robyn's voice on the other end. "I hope I'm not calling too early, but the kids and I want to meet you in an hour at the school playground. If that's OK with you, I'll stop by and we can go together."

"Sure!" Johnnie replied. Inwardly he was so excited he had to work hard to keep his voice even and calm. "By the way, my mom wondered if everyone would like to have lunch over here today."

There was a pause on the other end of the line. Johnnie began to worry that Robyn didn't want to come and was trying to think of a way to say no. When Robyn finally spoke she sounded surprised. "Are you sure?" she asked. There will be six of us—seven, including you!"

"I think that will be OK," Johnnie said. "Hold on a minute."

He put his hand over the mouthpiece and turned to his mother. "Mom, do you think you can handle seven of us for lunch?"

Mrs. Jacobson smiled. "Of course! We'll have hot dogs, chips, cookies and soda. It will be fun!"

Johnnie smiled appreciatively at his mother. She was like that—always willing to make things work.

Johnnie uncovered the mouthpiece and said, "No problem!"

"Great!" said Robyn. "I'll call everybody and tell them the plan. See you in about an hour! Bye!"

"Bye!" Johnnie replied. As he hung up the receiver, he had a feeling that everything was going to be more than just OK—it was going to be great.

At nine o'clock Robyn knocked on the Jacobsons' front door. Johnnie had seen her coming up the sidewalk and was right there to answer it. He grabbed the CD off his dresser and tucked it in the backpack on his wheelchair. He said good-bye to his mom and then skillfully wheeled down the ramp his father had built from the front porch to the sidewalk leading to their driveway.

The school was only three blocks from Johnnie's house. Johnnie's strong arms were able to push the wheelchair easily the whole distance. The other kids were already there.

Katy and Danny Randall ran to greet Johnnie and Robyn as they approached. Danny was 11 years old, like Johnnie. His sister Katy was 8 years old. Johnnie could tell from their blonde hair and tanned skin that these two liked being outdoors.

"Hi!" Danny yelled as he ran toward them. "We all just got here a few minutes ago. Did you remember to bring 'the item'?"

"Sure did!" Johnnie said as he patted the backpack.

"Well then," Danny said. "Let's get over to the other kids so we can get this initiation thing over with. Then we can have some fun! Do you play baseball?"

Katy looked at her brother and rolled her eyes. "That's all you ever think about. First I want to see what Johnnie found and hear what happened down at the barn."

By this time the other kids had joined them and formed a circle around Johnnie. Travis stood in front of Johnnie, his blue eyes looking past Johnnie at the baseball field. In one hand he held a baseball and in the other a baseball glove. It was obvious that he wasn't too interested in what Johnnie had found. He just wanted to get started with the game.

Next to Travis, 10-year-old Nick Tysman was squinting at Johnnie's wheelchair. He tilted his head to one side as he studied the wheels, hubs, shinny spokes and sleek, black frame. He had never seen a wheelchair like that one before. Johnnie almost laughed as he watched Nick's dark-brown eyes take in every inch of his chair. "Hey!" Nick blurted out. "How come your chair doesn't look like the ones in the grocery store?"

Johnnie smiled as he pictured the high-backed, chrome-plated wheelchairs that many retail stores kept on hand for their customers who needed them. They were basic wheelchairs designed for someone other than the rider to push.

At Nick's question, Joey Thomas' jaw dropped open. He stared hard at Nick in disbelief. Joey, like Katy, was 8 years old. His short brown hair, round face and rosy cheeks made him look almost like a cherub.

"Ni-ick!" Joey whispered, the color in his cheeks becoming a deeper pink, "Maybe Johnnie doesn't want to talk about his wheelchair."

Johnnie overheard Joey's comment and smiled at him, which made Joey flush even more in embarrassment. "Don't worry, Joey," Johnnie said. "I don't mind people asking questions."

Just then Travis shifted his stance and looked directly at Johnnie as he spoke to the rest of the group. "Look," he said abruptly, "we don't have all day to talk about wheelchairs. That's not why we're here. We're supposed to see whatever it was that Johnnie supposedly brought back from the barn and then get on with playing baseball. OK?"

"OK," Danny said, trying to soften Travis' harsh words a little. "We'll take a look at what Johnnie did find at the barn." He shot a glance at Travis to let him know he was being out of line. Travis rolled his eyes but remained quiet.

Ignoring Travis' sarcastic remark, Johnnie reached around to his backpack and opened it. Carefully he felt for the plastic CD case and pulled it out for everyone to see.

"What is it?" Nick asked.

"It's a CD!" said Danny excitedly. "Wow! It's the latest one by that new group, Jonah Whalen!"

"Jonah who?" Nick asked, scrunching up his nose.

"Oh, I've heard of them," said Katy. "They're a rock group. Danny has their first CD and was waiting for this one to come out."

"I'm just surprised it's out already!" Danny said. "Let's take it back to my house and listen to it."

"Wait a minute," Johnnie said holding out the CD case. "It's empty—see!" He opened it to show them. The folded paper cover was securely nestled inside the plastic sleeve. On it was the name of the CD and the lyrics, along with some small print that identified the members of the Jonah Whalen group.

"Wasn't there a CD somewhere near it?" asked Danny, disappointment showing in his eyes.

"No! The only thing I saw was the CD lid on the ground. It was kind of dark in there. Maybe I just didn't see it."

"Maybe you just didn't get it from there," Travis said. "That barn has been empty for 15 years. What would a CD be doing there—especially one that is so new?"

"Maybe it's a mystery!" Katy said, her eyes sparkling with the prospect of a new adventure.

"And maybe you read too much," Travis snapped back. "I'll bet if we check out Johnnie's bedroom we'll find the rest of the CD."

"Uh, I hate to shatter your theory, Travis, but Johnnie showed me that CD case when I went to find him down by the barn." Robyn's voice was stern and she raised herself to her full height as she glared at Travis, silently daring him to say something.

When the other kids all began looking at Travis, their hands on their hips, Travis backed down. "Well, OK," he said. "So he found a stupid CD case. Big deal. Now can we play baseball?"

Katy, who hadn't abandoned her mystery idea, asked Johnnie if she could see the CD lid. Holding it to her chest as if she were holding her teddy bear and looking in the direction of Gun Lake she said convincingly, "I just know there's a mystery here. What would a CD be doing down at the barn?"

Johnnie, who got caught up in Katy's enthusiasm, blurted out, "And that's not all!"

Suddenly he was the center of attention. Even Travis stopped tossing the baseball up in the air to look at him.

"When I was inside the barn looking for something to bring back, I noticed a secret door." The very words "secret door" sent chills of excitement through everyone's body. "I opened it," Johnnie continued. "It was pretty dim by then because the sun had gone down behind the dunes, but I could see what looked like stacks of something inside."

"Hey!" Danny said as he almost stumbled over Johnnie's wheelchair. "Maybe those are boxes full of Jonah Whalen CDs—and maybe the actual discs are inside them! I say let's go check it out."

"I say we'd better wait until this evening," Robyn said. "If those CDs belong to someone, I don't want to run into them while we're snooping around. We can bring flashlights."

"The barn door had been locked," Johnnie said. "But I could only find the chain in the dark and not the padlock. So it's open!"

Everyone looked at each other. Danny's breath came in short, excited bursts, but he agreed with Robyn. "OK," he said at last. "We go at eight o'clock this evening. There will still be enough light to see."

The group started to head toward the baseball field when Nick spoke up. "Uh, guys! Aren't we forgetting something? Just a little detail about voting Johnnie into the club?"

"Oh, right!" Danny said apologetically. "Sorry about that, Johnnie. In all the excitement I forgot why we really came here. Would you mind if we have a few minutes alone to vote?"

"No, not at all!" Johnnie said. He watched as the

group of kids walked away from him a short distance and huddled in a circle. Johnnie could hear them talking in low, murmuring voices, but he couldn't make out what they were saying. Then he saw them all put their right hands into the circle as they looked away to the outside of the circle. In a voice Johnnie could hear, Danny counted to three. Then everyone looked at their fingers. One finger out meant yes; two fingers meant no.

There was a loud cheer when the group counted the vote. Danny came running over to Johnnie exclaiming, "You're in!"

A big smile crossed Johnnie's face and he thought he was going to cry. Quickly he wheeled his chair toward the rest of the gang so Danny couldn't see his moist eyes. "Let's play ball!" he shouted.

Everyone but Travis cheered and began running toward the field. Travis just sighed as Johnnie rolled past him. "How are you going to play baseball?" he half muttered.

On the baseball field, Nick came up to Johnnie and ran his fingers over the black, shiny aluminum frame of Johnnie's chair. "Wow! This sure is a cool chair!" he said. "By the way, how do you play baseball from a wheelchair?"

"No problem!" said Johnnie. "I have someone who runs for me, but I can bat right from my chair. The pitcher just has to throw it a little lower, that's all. I used to play third base in California. I just don't use a glove so I can move my chair around."

"Awesome!" Nick said.

Because there were only seven of them, they had to modify their baseball game a little. They only ran to first base and back. After hitting the ball, the runner could stay on first base until the next batter hit the ball. There was a catcher, pitcher and first baseman in the field. Each team had three members. They all took turns playing the seventh position—outfield. Danny, Johnnie and Robyn ended up on team one—the "Awesome Three"— while Travis, Katy and Nick were on team two—the "Tidal Waves." Joey agreed to play outfield for the first inning.

The kids spent the better part of the morning playing baseball. Travis was the pitcher for the Tidal Waves. He pitched fast and hard. Johnnie struck out three times in a row. But he had better luck being first baseman. He surprised the kids by how well he could maneuver his wheelchair around the baseball field. Once, when Joey was playing outfield, Travis hit a grounder toward center field. Joey quickly scooped up the ball and threw it with all his might toward Johnnie who was at first base. The ball veered slightly to the right. Without hesitating, Johnnie pushed his chair so he would be in position to catch it, and then he wheeled as fast as he could toward first base just as Travis came sliding in. When the dust cleared, Johnnie was sitting coolly with one caster wheel firmly planted on the base, lightly tossing the ball in the air and catching it again. By the look on Travis face, the others knew Travis was out. The two boys looked at each other. Johnnie finally broke the silence. "Nice hit—but you're out of there!"

Without a word, Travis turned and jogged back toward the batter's box. He looked at his watch, grabbed the baseball and his glove and said, "I gotta go home for lunch."

"Wait a minute!" Robyn called after him as he began walking toward his house. "We're all invited to Johnnie's for lunch—remember?!"

Travis looked over his shoulder as he continued on his way. "Sorry. Gotta go!"

All faces turned toward Johnnie to see how he'd react. Inwardly, Johnnie was torn between making a sarcastic remark or begging Travis to come home with him. He watched Travis for a moment, then sighed. "Well," he said to the others, "let's go eat!"

Mrs. Jacobson had everything ready by the time the kids arrived. Hot dogs, cookies, soda and chips were neatly placed on the picnic table in their backyard. The hungry kids eagerly helped themselves and chatted. Mrs. Jacobson talked easily with the kids, but mostly she listened. Her smiling face and light laughter told Johnnie that she approved of his new friends.

After lunch Mrs. Jacobson cleared away the dirty dishes and extra food. Then she went into the house. Meanwhile, Katy wandered over to a lounge chair next to the house. She spotted that day's newspaper on the side table next to her. Katy, who had a habit of reading anything with words on it, casually lifted the paper to scan the headlines. Toward the bottom of the first page a headline caught her eye: "CD Pirating on the Increase."

CD pirating? Katy thought. I wonder if they mean compact discs?

Her curiosity compelled her to keep reading the article. As she read, her brown eyes popped open wide and her mouth formed a huge, silent "O."

"Hey everyone!" she yelled, barely able to contain her excitement. "Listen to this! FBI agents recently confiscated a shipment of illegally produced compact discs. The discs were part of a shipment found aboard a tanker that was docked in Chicago. Investigators believe the shipment originated in Hong Kong where other shipments of confiscated tapes and CDs have been seized. Robert Warren of the FBI investigating team said, 'Pirates get ahold of not-yet-released CDs and mass-produce them. They wait until the real CD is going to be released and then flood the market with copies. The fake CDs are sold at a lower cost and usually through catalog sales or at temporary booths set up at carnivals, shopping malls, etc.'"

Johnnie took out the CD lid he had found. Looking at it, he thought of the secret room and what looked like stacks of boxes. "I wonder. . ." he said half aloud.

Danny, Nick, Robyn and even Joey began to get caught up in Katy and Johnnie's adventuresome spirit. "I can't wait until eight o'clock this evening," Robyn said. "I just hope we don't get caught."

CHAPTER THREE

Tire Tracks!

JOHNNIE HURRIED THROUGH DINNER, THEN HELPED his mother clear the table. The late afternoon sun hung midway between straight up and the horizon. A few wispy clouds glazed the blue sky. Johnnie thought it would never get darker. After the kitchen had been put back in order, Johnnie wheeled outside to the backyard. The gentle lake breeze felt good against his warm face.

He checked his wristwatch. Two more hours until Robyn would come over and they would head for Gun Lake. What am I going to do until Robyn gets here? he wondered. The ringing of the telephone interrupted his thoughts. It was Danny. He asked Johnnie to bring over the CD so he could at least look at the lyrics printed on the cover. Apparently Robyn was already over there. Danny lived at the end of the block on the street just behind Johnnie. After checking with his parents, Johnnie took off down the sidewalk toward Danny's house.

Coming toward him on the street was a boy on a

bicycle. Before getting to Johnnie's block, however, the boy turned left on the cross street. "Hmmm," Johnnie mumbled to himself. "I wonder if that was Travis on his way to Danny's."

A few minutes later, Johnnie wheeled up to the breezeway at the Randall house. He rang the doorbell and waited. Then he heard voices coming from the backyard. Before anyone could answer the door, Johnnie wheeled to the backyard where he found Danny, Katy, Robyn, Nick, Joey and Travis. Katy and Nick were playing tetherball, while Joey watched. Danny, Robyn and Travis were starting to play a game of cards called "Uno."

Danny looked up and saw Johnnie sitting in the driveway watching them. "Hey! Johnnie! Come on in. Do you know how to play Uno?"

"No, I've never played that game before," Johnnie said. "But I suppose I can learn."

Travis didn't look up as Johnnie joined them at the round patio table.

"Did you bring the CD paper?" Danny asked.

Johnnie pulled the plastic lid with the cover paper still folded neatly and secure inside it. He handed it to Danny who opened it carefully. "Wow! Cool!" he said. "I can't wait to hear what these songs sound like."

Meanwhile, Robyn dealt the cards to the four players and tried to explain the game to Johnnie. "Don't worry," she said. "We'll play a practice round. You'll catch on."

Johnnie looked at Travis who was sitting across from him. Travis glanced up and saw Johnnie looking at him. "What are you looking at?" he snarled.

Robyn and Danny looked at each other, then Danny quickly spoke. "Oh, come on, Travis. Let's just play the game, OK?"

Travis didn't answer. When Robyn finished dealing out the cards he picked his up and began sorting them. Johnnie didn't say anything either. He picked up his cards and began putting them in order according to color.

After the practice round, he caught on quickly and became so engrossed in the game that he hardly noticed Travis. Johnnie, Danny and Katy laughed and talked while playing. Travis remained quiet. He didn't seem to be enjoying himself at all. When Danny was the first one to get rid of all his cards, Travis was the first one to leave the table. "I've had enough of Uno," he said as he sulked away.

Johnnie watched as Travis went over to where Katy and Nick were battling it out around the tetherball pole. He sighed, then turned to Danny who was also watching Travis. "Why doesn't he like me?" Johnnie said. "Is it because I'm in a wheelchair?"

Danny thought a moment before answering. "Well," he started slowly. "My dad says that Travis has a rough home life. His dad is a top executive at some company, and he travels all the time. Whenever he's home, all he's interested in is how many A's Travis got on his report card and how many touchdowns he scored or baskets he made or home runs he hit. Whenever Travis doesn't do what his dad thinks he should, well—my dad says his dad just expects a lot."

"Yeah, so what does that have to do with me?" Johnnie asked.

Danny sighed and shrugged his shoulders. "I don't know," he replied honestly.

"Well," Robyn said as she inched closer to the two boys. "I think Travis is a lot like his dad. His dad won't accept anything that isn't perfect and. . ." She suddenly stopped and blushed. "I-I'm sorry," she stammered. "I didn't mean to make it sound as if you were less than perfect."

Johnnie looked at Robyn a couple of seconds and then burst out laughing. Danny, who wasn't quite sure what to do, started laughing too. Robyn just looked from one boy to the other, half smiling and half looking bewildered.

"What gave you your first clue?" Johnnie asked, still chuckling.

"Uh, my first clue about what?" Robyn asked.

"Your first clue that I'm not perfect!" Johnnie said, now smiling broadly at the still-bewildered Robyn.

"Well—um, what I meant was nobody's perfect," Robyn said, feeling a little picked on.

Johnnie saw that Robyn was genuinely uncomfortable and he didn't want to make her angry with him. "It's OK, Robyn," he said. "You're right. I'm not perfect. You're not perfect. And you're probably right about Travis."

He paused for a moment and then added, "I just hope that someday Travis can see past my wheelchair and see the person sitting in it."

Just then Katy's loud, clear voice came at them from across the backyard. "I won!" she yelled. It had been one of the longest tetherball games she had ever played with Nick. They were pretty evenly matched. Nick managed to win the first two games, but Katy clinched the third.

Johnnie looked over at Nick who was sprawled on the grass face up and breathing hard. Katy sat down next to Nick. "Good game!" she said enthusiastically. "Now you're only one up on me!"

Travis, who had been sitting nearby watching them jump and slap the ball around the pole, suddenly got up, glancing at his watch. "Come on, everybody," he said. "If we're going to go down to the barn, I say let's do it now."

Robyn looked at her watch, noting that it was only 7:30 PM. It was a half hour before they had said they'd go down, but she was anxious to get going too. "Good idea," she said.

Travis led the way to the driveway that would take them to McGruther's barn. The other kids followed close behind. Danny and Robyn stayed close to Johnnie. "Do you still have that CD case?" Johnnie asked.

"I left it back at my house," said Danny. "For safekeeping," he added.

Swirls of clouds mixed with pinks and blues began to mingle in the early-evening sky. There was still plenty of light—especially by the lake. The shadows of the trees made the dirt driveway a little dim, but it was still light enough to easily see the old barn as they rounded the bend.

Travis and the others slowly walked alongside Johnnie as he wheeled his way to the barn. Johnnie pointed to the first set of doors. "When I realized these were locked, I wheeled around the side hoping to find another set of doors," he explained. He led the way around the side of the barn.

When they reached the other end, Johnnie stopped suddenly. The chain was in the door, just as he had left it. But there, threaded through the chain's links, was the padlock he had been unable to find the night before—only now it was securely locked.

Johnnie saw Travis roll his eyes. He knew Travis didn't believe that he had been in the barn. Just then Nick, who had wandered off toward the lake, shouted back to the others. "Hey! Come here! There are tire tracks!"

"They're probably just Johnnie's wheelchair tracks," said Katy.

"I don't think so," said Nick. "There are large footprints beside them, and they look as if they are going down the path that leads to the lake."

Quickly the kids scampered over to where Nick was standing. Sure enough, tire tracks and footprints were leading both to and from the lake.

"These tire prints are too close together to be from my wheelchair," Johnnie said, "and my front caster wheels are closer together than my back wheels."

"That's right!" said Danny excitedly. "If these had been wheelchair tracks, we'd see four tire marks!"

"Let's follow the tracks and see where they lead," Katy said excitedly, as she started off down the trail.

"Hey! Wait a minute," Danny called after her. "What if whoever made these tracks is still down there?"

Katy hesitated a moment to ponder her brother's

warning. More cautiously than before, she continued down the path. "Let's take it slow," she whispered back to the others.

Not willing to let his sister go by herself, Danny caught up with her. Nick, Joey, Travis, Robyn and Johnnie all followed behind.

CHAPTER FOUR

Camp Out
at Lookout Point?

FTER DISCOVERING THE FOOTPRINTS, THE "mystery of the CD" was all the kids could talk about. They felt sure that these CDs had something to do with the CD pirates Katy had read about in the newspaper, but they wanted to be sure before they let anyone else in on their mystery adventure. Somehow they needed to watch McGruther's barn without being detected.

"It's been exactly one week since we visited McGruther's barn," said Danny. "Whoever locked up the barn came last Friday. Maybe they'll be back again tonight."

"Well, we just can't go out in the woods and wait for them," said Robyn. "That would be too dangerous. What if we got caught?"

"I've got it! Let's have a camp out," said Danny. "We could all meet at Lookout Point, set up tents and keep watch.

You can see Gun Lake from up there as well as the channel from Lake Michigan. It would be perfect!"

Johnnie wasn't at all sure his parents would let him spend the night in some tent on a lookout point—at least not without some supervision. He didn't want to sound like he couldn't take care of himself, and he didn't want to make up some excuse as to why he couldn't go. While all the other kids were talking about what food they were going to bring, what games they could play and how cool it would be to spy on McGruther's barn, Johnnie just sat quietly.

Nick, who was sitting down next to Johnnie, began looking at the shiny spokes. "Hey!" he suddenly blurted. "How can you go camping in a wheelchair? Will you have to bring a hospital bed or something?"

Everyone became quiet, waiting for Johnnie to answer. "Well, I did go camping once with my youth group, but it was inside cabins," Johnnie answered quietly. "And no, I don't need a hospital bed, Nick. Once I transfer out of my wheel-chair, I can sleep on the ground in a sleeping bag."

"Transfer?" asked Nick. "What's that?"

"It just means getting from my wheelchair to somewhere else—like a chair or a bed or the ground," Johnnie answered.

"Well, we all have to go home and ask our parents about this," said Danny. "Just don't tell them the part about spying.

I'm hungry, and it's lunchtime. Let's all go home and then meet at the schoolyard in about an hour."

At home, Danny and Katy excitedly told their mother about their camping plans. This was something the neighborhood kids did once in a while. Lookout Point was about a mile away from Gun Lake, but the dune was high above Lake Michigan, giving a perfect view of the surrounding area—including Gun Lake. On these camping expeditions, Danny's father usually accompanied them. If not him, then one of the other parents supervised.

"You'll have to clear this with your dad," Mrs. Randall said. "He's probably available right now, if you want to call him at the office."

Danny quickly went over to the telephone and punched in the number to his dad's office. When his father's voice came on the phone, Danny told his dad about their camping plans. "Can we go, Dad? Can we? It's really important!"

"What's so important about going tonight?" Mr. Randall asked.

"Uh—well, it will be Johnnie's first camp out—and, well. . ." Danny stumbled around for an answer that would be honest but that wouldn't give the mystery away.

"Your new friend Johnnie is going camping too?" Mr. Randall asked, surprised. "Have his parents given him permission yet?"

"Well, we're all checking with our parents," said Danny. "But if you come with us, I'm sure it will be OK."

"I'm not sure I'd be able to take care of Johnnie's needs," said Mr. Randall. "Why don't you let me call Johnnie's parents and talk it over with them."

Thinking that was a good idea, Danny gave his dad the Jacobsons' phone number. Mr. Randall promised to call Johnnie's mom right away and then get back to his son when he got home from work. Danny was a little disappointed that he didn't get an answer right away, but he was hopeful everything would work out.

Meanwhile, Johnnie's mom had mixed feelings about her son's request to go with the other kids. On the one hand, she wanted him to fit in with his friends. But on the other hand, she had no idea if this Lookout Point was safe. Even Johnnie wasn't sure. All he knew is, he had to be there. If there was any pirate activity tonight, he wanted to see it first-hand.

"I'll talk it over with your father, when he gets home this evening," Mrs. Jacobson said. "I'm sorry I can't give you a yes or no answer right now," she added when she saw Johnnie's frustration. "This is sort of short notice. Your dad and I just need a chance to talk about it. OK?"

"Please say yes, Mom," Johnnie pleaded. "I really need to go. Please, please, please!"

Mrs. Jacobson smiled at her son. "I know this is important to you. Don't take my wanting to talk it over with your dad as a no—it's just a temporary 'maybe.' As soon as your dad and I can talk, we'll make a decision."

"Yeah, sure," Johnnie mumbled. Then looking at the clock, he realized he had only 10 minutes to make it to the schoolyard. "Gotta go, Mom!" Johnnie said. "I'll be home at dinnertime."

With that, he pushed his way out the door, down the ramp and off toward the school. When he got to the meeting place, most of the other kids were already there. He was dreading having to tell everyone that he wouldn't know if he could go until this evening.

"Hi!" Nick said, as Johnnie approached the group. "Are you going to be able to come camping?"

"Um, I'm not sure yet," Johnnie answered. He searched the others' faces to see what their reaction would be. Then he continued, "My mom needs to check it out with my dad, when he gets home this evening."

"Yeah, mine too," Joey said.

"My mom said I could go if there was an adult going along," said Nick. "My dad is on a business trip, so he won't be able to go."

Just then Danny and Katy joined the group. "Hi, guys!" they said.

Danny had heard Nick's statement, and said, "I think my dad's going to come." He glanced over at Johnnie, not sure if he should tell him that his dad wasn't sure if he could "take care of Johnnie's needs" or not. Deciding Johnnie would probably find out sooner or later, he turned to Johnnie and said, "My dad said he was going to call your parents to—you know—check things out with them."

Johnnie wasn't quite sure what that meant, but it made him feel a little uncomfortable. He didn't want to be the center of attention. He just wanted to go camping with the rest of them.

Just then Travis came bounding over to the group. "My mom said it would be OK," he said. "She just wants to make sure some adult is going to be there. You know how moms are."

"Yeah," everyone agreed.

The rest of the afternoon was spent planning—just in case everything worked out, and everyone could go. They would collect driftwood, set up a campfire on the dune, roast hot dogs and marshmallows and keep busy—all the while keeping a sharp eye on Gun Lake. It was decided that if they did see anything unusual, they would keep quiet about it— or at least just talk quietly among themselves.

"No sense in getting our parents involved—yet," Travis had said.

Later that afternoon everyone went home for dinner and to find out what the "verdict" would be. Danny could hardly wait until his father pulled up in the driveway.

Johnnie was equally anxious for his dad to come home. He had rehearsed in his mind all the reasons why he should be allowed to go. He could transfer out of his wheelchair himself. He was able to dress himself. Tying shoes was a little problem, so he'd wear his sandals. Knowing that his wheelchair would be hard to push in the sand, he figured he could have his dad bring up some plywood to make a temporary floor. He just had to make it work.

As soon as Johnnie heard his dad's car drive up, he was out the door, down the ramp and next to the driver's side of the car.

"Well!" Johnnie's father said, looking surprised. "This is quite the greeting! With a greeting like this, who needs a dog?"

"Da-ad," Johnnie said, shaking his head and smiling at his dad's attempt at humor.

"Wha-at?" Mr. Jacobson good-naturedly mocked him.

"Guess what?" Johnnie began.

"I don't know," his father said. "Let me guess. You want to go camping tonight?"

Johnnie's mouth dropped opened in surprise. "You-you know about it?" he asked.

Mr. Jacobson couldn't help but laugh at the bewildered look on his son's face. "Why, of course I know," he said teasingly. "Fathers know everything about their sons—just remember that!"

"How did you know about the camp out?" Johnnie insisted.

"Danny's father called your mother this afternoon to talk to her about letting you go on the camping trip. He explained that he normally accompanies the kids on their trips, and wondered if I'd be interested in coming along. Your mom gave him my work phone number, he called, and well—I guess we're going camping!"

Johnnie was stunned. He had never considered having his father come along. Inwardly he felt a huge sense of relief. Even though he had been prepared to brave this camping trip by himself, he was a little fearful that he might need some help and would be too embarrassed to ask. Now, he wouldn't have to worry, and he wouldn't have to put up with any remarks from Travis— although he had to admit that, while Travis wasn't exactly friendly yet, he had stopped rolling his eyes every time Johnnie said something. In fact,

Travis seemed just as excited about this mystery as all the others.

Suddenly Johnnie was aware that his dad was waiting for some kind of response to the news he had just shared with him. He also became aware that he had unconsciously been holding his breath. With one huge exhale, Johnnie started breathing again. A smile as wide as a football field spread across his face as he reached out to give his dad a big hug. Mr. Jacobson kneeled down beside Johnnie's wheelchair to receive the hug.

"Well, I guess this means it's OK with you if I tag along," Mr. Jacobson said with a smile.

"Yeah," Johnnie said, then added: "It's more than just OK. It's great!"

"Before we go, we need to go to the medical supply store," Mr. Jacobson said with a mischievous look in his eye.

"Medical supply store?" Johnnie asked, scrunching up his nose. "I don't need any special supplies!"

"Trust me!" was all his dad said as they wheeled out to the family van.

"We'll be back in about a half hour," Mr. Jacobson called out to his wife, as he and Johnnie pulled out of the driveway.

"When are we supposed to meet at Lookout Point?" Johnnie asked, a little worried that they might be late.

"Mr. Randall set the time for seven o'clock," Mr. Jacobson answered. "Danny, Katy and Travis will ride up in the Randalls' car. Nick, Joey and Robyn will ride up with you and me in our van. Don't worry. We'll have plenty of time—and I'm sure you'll agree that this little trip will be worth it."

When Johnnie and his dad arrived at the store, Mr. Jacobson used the van's specially built power lift to lower Johnnie, who was securely strapped in his wheelchair, down to the parking lot. Johnnie's father unhooked the straps that had held the chair in place and Johnnie wheeled himself out of the van.

Inside the store, Mr. Jacobson introduced himself to the man behind the counter.

"Glad to meet you, Mr. Jacobson. My name is Jim Switzer. I'm the one you talked to earlier. Your dune chair is all ready."

"Your what?" Johnnie asked. He had never heard of a dune chair.

"If you're going to be able to get around on that sand dune, you are going to need a chair with special balloon tires," Mr. Jacobson explained. "We're renting one for the weekend!"

"Here it is!" Jim said, as he wheeled out a chair that had huge tires with no tread.

Johnnie reached over to feel the tires. "They feel like they need air," Johnnie said.

"Actually, they have just the right amount of air in them," Jim replied. "We have found that the harder the tire is—the more air it has in it—the more difficult it is to push in sandy soil."

"Wow! Cool!" Johnnie said. "Can I go anywhere on the dune in this?"

"Well, just about," Jim said with a smile. "You don't want to go down the side of one of those 100-foot dunes! Gradual slopes are OK. But just remember—if you go down you're going to have to come up!"

Johnnie looked at his dad and grinned. "Thanks, Dad! I never would have thought of this!"

Back home, Johnnie and his dad ate dinner and got packed. Mrs. Jacobson helped load their gear into the van and then kissed them both good-bye. They picked up their three passengers and were on their way.

The trip up to Lookout Point took less than 10 minutes. The first task was to unload the vehicles and set up the tents. The kids were amazed at Johnnie's dune chair, and

Nick could hardly contain himself. "Can I ride in it?" he asked.

"Tell you what," Mr. Jacobson said. "When we're all sitting around the campfire, you can take it for a spin!"

"Yes!" Nick said. "Let's get that campfire going!"

Johnnie helped the kids gather firewood. He wheeled alongside Nick and Joey and carried in his lap the driftwood they gathered. The others busied themselves with organizing the supplies, finding large stones to form a fire pit and going into the nearby woods to gather dried twigs and small branches for kindling. For good measure, Mr. Randall had brought several good-sized logs from his own backyard woodpile. "These will burn for hours," he said.

Even with everyone helping, it took well over an hour to get everything organized. Mr. Randall and Mr. Jacobson decided to let the kids handle as much of the setting up as possible. Because both men had discovered that each enjoyed fishing, they packed reels, rods, tackle and ice chests.

After the tents had been pitched and everyone was settled, Mr. Randall took Mr. Jacobson to the edge of Lookout Point. Pointing north, he showed Mr. Jacobson a portion of the beach on Lake Michigan where an abandoned building was silhouetted against the evening sky. The building itself was on a flat piece of land, now overgrown with dune grass. Surrounding it on three sides was a wall of boulders. It jutted out from the shoreline about 20 feet and was about 10 feet high.

"That used to be part of the old water filtration plant," Mr. Randall said. "A few years ago, they built a new plant farther up the coast. A lot of fishermen still like to come to this spot and do some offshore fishing. While the kids are up here playing games and talking, we can go down and take a look. If we get up first thing in the morning, we should have a pretty good chance of catching something—that is, if Johnnie would be OK for a short time by himself."

Mr. Jacobson smiled, then looked at the place where Mr. Randall had been pointing. "I'm sure Johnnie will be just fine. It's only a short distance from here, and actually, Johnnie is pretty independent."

"I hope you don't mind my asking about Johnnie," Mr. Randall said. "I've never had to deal with anyone who has a disability, and quite frankly, I don't know what to expect."

"Actually, I'm glad you're up front about it," Mr. Jacobson said. "I wouldn't expect you or anyone else who has never known someone with a disability to understand everything. And, the thing is, each person who has a disability is different. Some, like Johnnie, get around well. Johnnie is bright, active and enjoys the things other kids like. Then there are those who need some extra help with writing, communicating, taking care of themselves or getting around.

Most people don't understand or are embarrassed to ask questions. They assume that being in a wheelchair makes the person strange or stupid."

"Well, Danny and Katy have sure taken to Johnnie," Mr. Randall said. "And by the looks of all the talking and activity over there," he said, pointing to the kids who were still preparing for the campfire, "the kids all feel OK with one another. I am glad you came along—not just because of Johnnie—but it's nice just getting to know you."

With that they joined the kids and helped make the final preparations. The ice chest containing the sodas and hot dogs was placed conveniently close to the fire pit. That way, they could easily "dig in" when they became hungry or thirsty.

By now the sun was heading toward the horizon. The dazzling golden sky was clear except for a few feathery clouds that hung lazily around the sun. It was going to be a clear night. The gentle lake breeze stirred the air and rustled through the dune grass. The waves of Lake Michigan left their prints upon the shore as they rhythmically ebbed and flowed. They sounded like the wind as it used to blow through the mountain pines back in California.

Johnnie was caught up in the peaceful beauty of the majestic sunset. He had watched the sun slip beneath the horizon almost every night they had been in Michigan, and it seemed to him that each display of color was different than any other. He loved the way the lake mirrored the colors in the sky. If the lake was rough and the waves were choppy, the colors seemed to dance and flicker. But on nights like this one, the nearly still lake drank in the color and gently offered it back to the sky above. Johnnie thought he could stay there forever.

"Let's get this fire going," Nick yelled. "I want some marshmallows—and I want a ride!" The sharp sound of his voice cut through Johnnie's daydreaming and brought his thoughts back to the adventure ahead.

Mr. Jacobson lit the kindling and before long, a fire was blazing. They all sat around the glowing light, ate, told stories and talked. Mr. Jacobson and Mr. Randall decided to explore the fishing site, and so left the kids to themselves.

After Johnnie was comfortably settled in his sandy seat near the fire, Nick jumped into the wheelchair. He was smaller than Johnnie and so his feet didn't quite reach the footrests. "Hey!" he yelled. "How do you get this thing started?"

"Either have someone push you, or push on the top of the wheel with the heels of your hands. Once you get rolling, it will be easier," Johnnie answered.

Nick grunted and groaned and finally managed to get the chair moving. He rolled only a few feet forward when he stopped. Leaning back in the chair and breathing hard, he said, "Whew! This is harder than it looks. Will somebody pleeease push me?"

"Well, I would, but you're using my legs!" Johnnie said jokingly.

Everyone started laughing—except Travis. He just got up from his spot, walked over toward Nick and said, "Here! I'll push you. Where do you want to go?"

"Just wheel me around the campsite—but not too close to the edge!" Nick replied, surprised that it was Travis who had volunteered to push him.

Travis pushed Nick around the circumference of the dune a couple of times. When Nick finally got out of the chair, Travis parked it where it had been originally— a little to the left of and behind Johnnie. He had been quiet throughout Nick's ride, and only mumbled "You're welcome" when Nick had thanked him. Rejoining the group, Travis remained quiet, as if deep in thought.

Once the sun had begun its descent into the western sky, darkness seemed to come quickly. Johnnie looked up. Millions of stars looked like countless bright flashlights blinking down at him. Out on the lake, Johnnie could see the distant lights of boats. Most of them were small boats coming in after a day's fishing. There were larger ships too— perhaps a freighter carrying its cargo through the Great Lakes and eventually out through the St. Lawrence Seaway, which connected the Great Lakes to the Atlantic Ocean. Many of the boats out there were huge yachts—some of them large enough to sail on the ocean. Johnnie wondered if one of those ships far off on the horizon might be the "pirate ship" all of them hoped to see.

Finally the sun settled beneath the horizon. The cool lake breeze caused the air to become chilly; however, the warmth of the fire was sufficient. Soon the two dads were back at camp, excited about the prospects of arising early and trying their luck at fishing.

Inside their tent, Mr. Jacobson helped Johnnie prepare for their "adventure in camping," as Mr. Jacobson called it. He opened Johnnie's sleeping bag so all Johnnie would have to do is crawl in, cover himself with the open flap and zip the bag shut. Since all the kids were going to sleep in their T-shirts and shorts, the problem of changing into pajamas was eliminated. Katy and Robyn decided they would share a tent. Danny would camp out with his dad, and Travis, Joey and Nick agreed to sleep in the largest tent. Johnnie and his dad would occupy the tent closest to the path that led to the road. With all the sleeping arrangements made, the two fathers crawled into their own tents and settled in for the night. "Don't stay up too late," Mr. Randall called out. "And keep the noise down to a low roar—please!"

Danny and Katy had brought the Uno game—a perfect choice because they could all play. For the next two hours, the kids were engrossed in the game, speaking in loud whispers. Even Travis had joined in the conversation and was having a good time.

It was about 11:30 PM when Nick noticed a large yacht coming toward Gun Lake. "Look!" he shouted. After a chorus of "Shhhhhhhh," everyone looked in the direction Nick was pointing. The yacht was easily visible, and it was still about a mile away. For awhile it looked as if it might pass by.

"Probably on its way north to Ludington, Michigan," said Travis.

But then it became obvious that the yacht was slowing down—coming to a halt. The short channel to Gun Lake was certainly too narrow and shallow for a yacht that size to pass through. From their vantage point, they could see people moving around toward the back of the yacht. Because water is an excellent conductor of sound, they heard distinctive voices, but couldn't quite make out what was being said.

To everyone's surprise, once the crewmen had shut off the yacht's engines, another motor started. It sounded like a small motorboat. Sure enough, coming from behind the great yacht, a motorboat maneuvered alongside it. Small spotlights were lit and aimed at the smaller boat. The kids could clearly see that someone was unloading boxes from the yacht and handing them to two men who were in the motorboat.

In a few minutes, the motorboat took off toward the channel leading to Gun Lake. Everyone held their breath. No one dared speak, lest they be overheard. Travis and Danny went about quickly extinguishing the fire. They all waited in quiet anticipation.

Six, seven, eight times the motorboat made its way into and out of the channel. It was nearly 1:30 AM before the crew secured the tow rope from the motorboat to the yacht and once again headed out into the darkness of Lake Michigan.

Wordlessly, the kids watched the ship's lights grow smaller and fainter on the horizon. Finally, they disappeared from sight altogether. The kids looked at each other, and an understanding passed among them. They nodded. Tomorrow they would make another visit to the barn at Gun Lake.

CHAPTER FIVE

The Secret Room

JOHNNIE AWAKENED SLOWLY TO THE MUFFLED SOUND of footsteps and distant voices. It took him a moment to remember where he was. A quick look at the inside of the tent jogged his memory and he sat up still groggy. What time is it? he wondered.

Just as he unzipped his sleeping bag, his father opened the tent flap and poked his head inside. "Well!" he said cheerfully. "Glad to see you're awake! Mr. Randall and I caught a few fish and we're ready to start breakfast. You hungry?"

The idea of having breakfast out on the dune in the cool morning sun made Johnnie's stomach rumble in anticipation.

"What's for breakfast?" he asked.

"We brought some bacon, eggs, orange juice and donuts, and now we have fresh fish too!" his father replied.

Mr. Jacobson helped his son climb out of the sleeping bag and tent and into the wheelchair parked outside. The other kids stumbled out of their tents and yawned and stretched their way to the outdoor "kitchen" by the fire pit.

Mr. Randall had carefully placed a cooking rack on top of the stones in the pit to form an outdoor stove. The fire crackled as small flames flickered playfully under the two iron skillets that were placed on top of the rack. The delicious aroma of the cooking bacon, fish and eggs was hungrily breathed in by everyone. And when it was cooked and served, everyone attacked the food like a pack of sharks on a feeding frenzy. The only things left were the skeletons of the fish. Lying back on the sun-warmed sand, Johnnie was sure it didn't get any better than this.

Soon, however, it was time to clean their campsite, pack up and go home. It had been such a great night that every-one—even Mr. Jacobson and Mr. Randall—was already talking about camping out again before the summer came to an end.

In the parking area, Nick watched wide-eyed as the Jacobsons' van door opened and the lift was lowered. Johnnie carefully wheeled his chair onto the waiting lift. Mr. Jacobson flipped the control switch and the lift slowly rose until it was level with the open van door. Johnnie wheeled inside, locked the wheels in place and transferred to the captain's seat that had been made especially for him. He fastened his seat belt while his father loaded the wheelchair into the back of the van.

Before the two vehicles departed, the kids agreed to meet later that afternoon at the schoolyard to discuss the next step.

All the way home, Johnnie's mind sought to remember in detail the exciting events that had taken place the night before. Once home, he wheeled himself into his bedroom and began to imagine ways they could get into the barn. Surely, whoever had delivered those boxes the night before had securely locked the doors. *Hmmmm. Maybe there's a way to get in through the window at the top of the barn—the hayloft!* Johnnie considered the possibility. He hadn't paid too much attention to the roof or the open hayloft that first night he had been there. *I mean, it's not like I planned to climb up there or anything!* he said to himself with a little laugh.

"Hey! How was the camping trip?" Mrs. Jacobson asked, interrupting Johnnie's thoughts. She came into his room and waited for his response.

"Oh! It was great, Mom!" Johnnie answered. "That special dune chair was awesome. You should have seen Nick in it!" He laughed, remembering how helpless Nick had looked when the chair wouldn't move. Then he suddenly stopped laughing and frowned.

"What is it?" his mother asked.

"Oh, nothing," Johnnie answered. Realizing his mother wasn't about to leave until he explained, he said, "Well, just now I was thinking about how funny Nick looked when he tried to make my dune chair move. He just sat there huffing and puffing. He *did* manage to get it to go forward a little, but then he couldn't go any farther without help."

Johnnie took a deep breath and looked down at the floor. "All of a sudden I realized that *I* sometimes look helpless too. Maybe that's why Travis doesn't like me. Maybe to him, *I* look like Nick looked. Come to think of it, it was Travis who ended up pushing Nick around in that chair. Why do you think he did that?"

Mrs. Jacobson knelt down beside Johnnie and placed her arm around his shoulders. "It's hard to know what someone else is thinking," she said. "People often react to situations or other people without really knowing why themselves. Until they *want* to know why, or until they *want* to change how they react, there's not much you or anyone else can do. You must be who you are, Johnnie. If to some people you look helpless in that wheelchair—don't worry about it. By just being who you are, those people who are willing to see *you* and not just your wheelchair will soon find out that you're anything but helpless! Instead of focusing on Travis, why not enjoy the friendships you have with the other kids?"

"Yeah, I guess you're right," Johnnie said. "I just wish Travis liked me, that's all."

"Give him some time," Mrs. Jacobson said. "Instead of concentrating on the way you *wish* things were, take advantage of the way things *are!* And now, I think you'd better take a shower and get the sand out of your hair. Rest up for a while, and I'll call you in time for lunch."

Though he knew his mother was right, Johnnie couldn't help but feel a twinge of sadness when he thought about Travis. If only there was *some* way he could "prove" himself. In the meantime, he decided he would take his mother's advice and enjoy his friendships with Danny, Katy, Nick, Joey and Robyn.

After his bath, Johnnie put on some clean clothes and plopped himself down on top of his bed. The day was becoming hot and humid. Even the lake breeze seemed to have run out of batteries. Johnnie reached over to his nightstand to click on the small fan. He closed his eyes and began to visualize how he and the other kids could gain access to the barn. He wondered what they would do once they got inside. Would they find boxes and boxes of pirated CDs? If so, would they take a few to show the police? Would the police even believe them?

Suddenly he sat up. "Maybe we should tell our parents about this," he murmured. Then he let his head hit the pillow again. "Nah! If we did, they'd either tell us our imaginations were working overtime or they wouldn't let us go down there."

Despite the gnawing feeling that *some* adult should know about their upcoming adventure, Johnnie convinced himself not to involve any parents—at least not until they could *prove* something was going on.

By two o'clock, big gray clouds had started to work their way inland from the lake. Off in the distance, it sounded like thunder. Johnnie could see the leaves of the huge oak trees flutter as the wind gained speed. "Oh, no!" he said. "If it storms, we won't be able to go down to the barn."

Quickly he dialed Danny's phone number. When Danny answered, Johnnie asked if everyone was still planning to meet at the schoolyard.

"Well *I* am!" Danny replied. "And I think we'd better hurry. I'll call the others and tell them to meet us in 15 minutes."

When Johnnie arrived at the schoolyard, Danny, Katy and Robyn were already there. "Where are the others?" Johnnie asked.

"Nick's mom wanted him to go shopping with her and Joey is still sleeping," Danny answered. "I called Travis, but there was no answer, so it looks like it's just the four of us."

"What will we do if it storms?" Johnnie asked.

"We'll go another time," said Katy, matter-of-factly. "But I don't think it's going to storm—and even if it does, afternoon storms usually don't last long."

"I've been thinking," Johnnie said, and then paused. "Maybe we should wait until evening to go back to the barn."

Danny squatted next to Johnnie's wheelchair and plucked a blade of grass from the lawn. He twirled it in his fingers and then looked up at Johnnie. "Well," he said thoughtfully, "if we *did* wait, there would be a better chance that *all* of us could go!"

For some reason Johnnie couldn't explain, he felt convinced that *all* of them should go to the barn *that night*. He wheeled his chair back and forth, glancing anxiously at the massive gray clouds that appeared to be devouring the blue sky. A loud booming thunderbolt jolted the kids. Soon the pounding sounds of the lake mixed with the wind howling through the pine trees made conversation almost impossible.

As a dazzling white flash of lightning pierced the sky, Johnnie yelled, "I think we'd better get out of here!"

The first drops of rain began to pelt the earth. "I think you're right!" Robyn yelled back. Without asking whether Johnnie wanted help, Robyn grabbed onto the push handles of his wheelchair and began to run. "Let's all go over to your house, Danny," she shouted.

Danny and Katy ran on ahead with Robyn and Johnnie close behind. What started out as a few huge drops of water, soon felt like someone had turned on a zillion showers all at one time. Hair matted with rain, clothes clinging to wet bodies, the kids dashed and splashed their way to the Randall house.

Mrs. Randall greeted them with bath towels. Panting from the cold and sheer excitement of his "wild water" wheelchair ride, Johnnie blinked the water out of his eyes and asked breathlessly, "Do you have an old towel I could use to dry off my chair? If I don't dry it off, it'll be like the Tin Man after awhile," he added with a grin.

As it turned out, the storm bashed its way in from the lake and then quickly moved on. The lingering gray clouds were soon pushed aside by what seemed to be an even hotter sun than what was there before.

"Do you think it will be too muddy to go to the barn tonight?" Johnnie asked, his voice soft and strained.

"No, it won't be muddy," Danny reassured him. "The soil around here is so sandy that the water gets soaked up quickly. No, it's not mud I'm worried about."

"What are you worried about?" Johnnie asked.

"Mosquitos," Danny said, making a face. "I hate mosquitos."

"Everyone had better wear bug repellent," Robyn said, unconsciously scratching her arm, "especially if we're going down to the barn at night."

***

The sun was still high above the horizon when seven o'clock rolled around. Dry, fed, heavily perfumed with bug repellent and packing flashlights, everyone—including Travis, Joey and Nick—began a brisk walk toward the road that would lead them to McGruther's barn. As they neared the road, their pace slackened, and they became quiet. The question of how they were going to get inside the barn had not yet been resolved.

Once on the winding road, Johnnie noticed how the golden setting sun made the tree trunks look as if they had been coated in melted butter. If this weren't such a scary mission, he thought he'd just like to sit there and watch as Mother Nature put her woods to bed. Up ahead of him Travis walked—his shoulders strong and his back straight.

With his eye fixed on Travis' back, Johnnie broke the silence. "I wonder if someone could somehow get up onto the roof of the barn and then lower himself in through the hayloft window?"

Danny looked at Johnnie as if he were going to respond, and then seeing Johnnie was gazing steadily at Travis, said, "Yeah! I wonder if anyone of us could do that?"

By this time, the kids had rounded the last bend, and the barn stood clearly in sight. Travis, who appeared not to be listening, quickened his pace and jogged on ahead of the rest of the group. By the time the others caught up, Travis was already inspecting the barn doors. "They're locked," he said, walking back toward the group. "But I did notice a rather large oak tree growing off to the side over there," he said, pointing toward the far side of the barn. "I bet I could climb up there and swing out onto the roof from one of the branches."

Johnnie smiled to himself. "Great idea!" he said.

Without a word, Travis scrambled up the gnarled trunk of the tree and, almost squirrel-like, began climbing higher into its branches. The largest branch that hung over the roof was as thick as a man's arm toward the trunk, but then narrowed gracefully toward its tip. From the ground, all eyes were on Travis as he eased himself out over the roof, the branch bending under his weight. At first there was only the sound of Travis' body moving through the leaves. Then the rustling gave way to a crunching noise, like someone was chewing on fresh crackers. Unconsciously, everyone held their breath. Even Travis had stopped crawling and listened intently at the sound, which seemed to be coming from behind him. Robyn, who had moved directly under the outstretched limb, suddenly realized what was happening and froze. Forcing her mind to ignore the urge she had to panic, Robyn yelled to Travis, "Jump! The branch is breaking!"

Travis reacted as if someone had stuck him with a needle. He sprang from the branch toward the roof. The force of the leap caused the branch to give way. With one swift movement, Robyn jumped toward the opposite side of the tree. Its large trunk protected her from the branch as it crashed to the ground.

Everything happened so quickly that the other kids didn't know if they should look up to see whether Travis had made it or look over to see if Robyn had been flattened! Fortunately, Travis' jump was as successful as Robyn's.

By now the sun was being quickly pulled into the lake—or so it seemed. Travis lost no time in climbing to the top of the roof and inching his way on hands and knees toward the peak. Looking over the edge, he could see the open hayloft window just a few feet below him. Slowly turning himself around, he lowered himself over the edge until the toes of his shoes touched the bottom of the window. Suddenly, it occurred to him that he had not bothered to check to see if the hayloft had an upper floor. Suspended between the window and the roof's peak, Travis had no choice but to "take the plunge."

When his legs slid onto the rough boards that served as the flooring for the hayloft, Travis sighed with relief. He scrambled to his knees, took out the flashlight he had tucked into his jean's pocket and peered out through the window. Smiling down at his friends' worried faces, he said, "Everything's OK! It's still a little light in here, so I'll head down to investigate that room." Pausing a few seconds, he looked at Johnnie and asked, "Uh, where is it?"

Johnnie pictured the layout of the barn in his mind, then said, "When you get down to ground level, go toward the rear barn doors. It will be along the wall on your left, between the stalls and the door. You'll have to look carefully because the hinges are on the inside, which makes it look like part of the wall. There's a little knothole you can use to open the door."

"We'll keep watch out here," Danny said. "Be careful but hurry! I want to be out of here before it gets dark."

Travis nodded, then ducked his head back inside. The old wooden beams were thick with dust and cobwebs. Small piles of hay hugged the corners of the loft. About six feet away, there appeared to be a square hole. Upon investigating, Travis saw that it opened to the steps leading to the barn's main floor. Carefully, he lowered himself. The rungs of the wooden ladder creaked under his weight. Once on the ground, Travis aimed his flashlight toward the wall Johnnie had mentioned. As he inched closer, he noticed the knothole. Sure enough, there it was—the door to the secret room.

Travis stood there a few minutes staring at the door, his hand poised to open it. His breathing came a little harder and quicker. The palms of his hands were moist. With one deep breath, Travis swallowed and then quickly opened the door. He jumped back, afraid someone or something would jump out at him. But he was greeted with nothing but dark silence.

Assured that he was alone in the barn, he directed the flashlight beam into the room. Stacks of cardboard boxes greeted his eyes. The markings on the box were not in English. In fact, they weren't even recognizable letters. "This looks like Chinese or something," he said aloud. The boxes were stacked neatly almost all the way to the ceiling. Inching his way down the narrow aisles, Travis tried to count how many there were while he kept an eye out for any markings or labels that he could read.

Outside, the kids decided to put scouts in various locations. Robyn and Katy were stationed in the woods. Joey and Nick crouched down behind the sand dune that overlooked Gun Lake. Danny and Johnnie stayed near the barn in case Travis reappeared. Even with all the insect repellent the kids had sprayed on themselves, mosquitos were still buzzing around their heads.

By the lake, the sky was still a light blue with evening shades of gold and pink hovering above the horizon. In the woods it was dim, and the trees cast long dark shadows. The earlier storm had stirred up Lake Michigan, making the waves big and foamy. Joey and Nick found themselves almost yelling to be heard over the constant roar of the lake as the waves splashed onto the shore. For this reason, and because they had grown tired of staring at the water, the boys didn't hear the approaching motorboat until it was almost at the shoreline.

Joey and Nick scrambled down the back side of the dune, keeping their heads low. A surge of panic arose in each of them. Their legs felt as though they were chained to weights. Finally, Nick forced his legs into a run, and he sped past Joey as fast as he could toward the barn. It didn't take Joey long to catch up.

"Danny! Johnnie!" they both yelled out. "They're coming! The boat—it's here! NOW!"

"Oh, no!" Johnnie said. "We've got to get Travis out of there!"

Wheeling to the back doors of the barn, Johnnie cupped his hands and yelled through the cracks, "TRAVIS! You have to get out now! They're coming!"

Travis, who was still inspecting boxes deep inside the room, didn't hear him.

CHAPTER SIX

Trapped!

"JOHNNIE, WE'VE GOT TO GET OUT OF HERE," Danny whispered loudly, tugging at his wheelchair. "They're coming up the path."

Johnnie shot a quick look back toward the dune, cupped his hands once more and whispered as loudly as he could through the barn doors, "Travis! They're coming!"

Danny grabbed the push handles on Johnnie's wheelchair and ran as fast as he could toward the road. Nick and Joey were already ahead of them, warning Robyn and Katy to find good hiding places.

Realizing his wheelchair was as obvious as a billboard sign on a highway, Johnnie quickly scanned the woods for a suitable hiding place. "Over there!" he said breathlessly, as he pointed to a large clump of blackberry bushes. Danny pointed the chair in the direction of Johnnie's finger and plunged through fallen tree limbs, dead leaves and thorny branches until they were well behind the dense towering bushes. Danny was trembling, his eyes wide with fear. From their vantage point they could see the front of the barn where the hayloft was. They could also see two men in jeans and sports shirts walking up the sandy path that led from the dune to the barn.

Breathing hard, Danny gripped the armrest of the wheelchair. "What are we going to do?" he gasped. "We've got to get Travis out of there!"

***

Inside the secret room, Travis decided to open one of the boxes and take a look. He pried open a loose corner on one of the cartons resting on the ground. Carefully, he worked at the edges from around the side—just open enough to slip his hand inside. Something hard, smooth and cool met his fingertips. "A CD case!" Travis said out loud.

He managed to grasp the edge of one of the plastic cases between his thumb and forefinger. Using his other hand as a brace, he was able to pull out the case. "Jonah Whalen!" he said as he looked at the cover. He quickly opened the case. Sure enough, a shiny silver disc was nestled securely inside. "Wait'll the guys see this!" he exclaimed. He tucked the CD inside his shirt and made his way back out to the main room. Just as he was shutting the door to the secret room, he heard someone rattling the lock outside.

He was just about to call out to his friends, when the

sound of a man's voice stopped him cold. In a flash he realized he was in great danger of being discovered. As quietly as he could, Travis made a dash for one of the stalls on the far side of the barn. Without thinking, he slid inside and covered himself with as much straw as he could find.

The sound of the chain being loosened preceded the creaking of the opening barn doors. Travis peered out from his straw fortress and could see the unmistakable streams of light generated by powerful flashlights.

"Grab one of these dollies," a gruff voice said. "I'll open up the room and pass the boxes out to you. I figure we can haul about four of these at a time back to the ship."

"Four!" the other man said. His voice sounded younger. "We'll be doing this all night, at that rate."

"Yeah? Well, the sooner you stop yapping and get to work, the sooner we'll be finished."

Travis heard the man open the door to the secret room. In a few minutes, he could hear him shuffling around. Then with a grunt, he lowered a box onto the waiting dolly. "There's two dollies here, so you take two boxes and I'll take two boxes."

Oh, good, thought Travis. When they load up their boxes and head back to the boat, I'll get out of here.

Just then, the man with the gruff voice said, "Hey! Look

at this! This box has been opened, and it looks like someone has pulled a CD right out of the stack!"

Travis held his breath. His heart began beating so hard he was sure the men would be able to hear it. *Of all the boxes I would have to find!* Travis thought to himself, the fear rising inside of him.

"You're right," the younger man said. "Somebody's been in here all right. How do you think he got in?"

Horrified, Travis saw the beams of light flicker around the room. "Hey! There's a ladder leading up to the hayloft," the man with the gruff voice said.

In an instant, the two men ran across the barn floor and scrambled up the ladder. The stall in which Travis was hiding was directly below the loft. He could see beams of light filter through the large cracks in the hayloft's flooring.

A part of Travis wanted to bolt out of the stall and head for the open barn doors. Another part of him was so frightened that he was afraid to blink his eyes. Just as he thought he'd try for the door, the man with the gruff voice grumbled, "There's nothing up here. He could have come in through the window here and left the same way. We'd better look around inside and out before we go back to the ship. The boss isn't going to like this!"

As the men were coming down the ladder, the younger one suddenly said, "What's that smell?"

"I don't smell anything," the other man said. "Just smells like an old barn to me."

"No, it's not just the barn," the younger man insisted. "It smells like . . . like insect repellent."

Suddenly Travis realized that the bug repellent he had so generously sprayed on himself was giving off a silent signal.

"So what are you saying?" the other man said.

"I'm saying," the younger man said steadily, "that whoever was here was wearing insect repellent, and he's either still here, or he just recently left."

"I'll take a look around in here," said the man with the gruff voice. "You take a look outside."

Travis shut his eyes as the flashlight beam slowly scanned the inside of the barn. One by one, he could hear the man open the stall doors and look inside. He heard him kicking straw around. Sweat trickled down Travis' forehead and stung his eyes. Stay calm, he told himself. Don't make any movements.

The sound of footsteps drew closer. Travis could hear the man's heavy breathing. It would be only a matter of minutes before the stall door opened and the man would step inside. Travis made himself as small as he could and waited.

CHAPTER SEVEN

The Diversion

A
S SOON AS DANNY SAW THE MEN GO INSIDE THE barn, he ran over to where Robyn and Katy had been hiding. Joey and Nick were close by. Wordlessly, he motioned for the girls to follow him back to where Johnnie was hiding.

"We've got to come up with a plan to get Travis out of there," Danny said, his tone of voice serious.

"I know what to do," Johnnie said without hesitation.

"OK," Robyn said. "What's your plan?"

"We've got to get down to the beach, get that motorboat and take it to the other side of Gun Lake. The men will hear the boat's motor and come looking. Hopefully, Travis hasn't been found yet, and he'll be able to escape. If not, then the rest of you will have to go inside the barn and rescue him."

"The rest of us?" Danny asked. "Where will you be?"

"I'll be in the boat," Johnnie answered, giving Danny a steady look. "I figure that with the plywood boards in place,

I can wheel down to the boat just about as fast as anyone else can. I'm good at boating, and I don't know how much help I'd be in rescuing Travis from the barn."

"I'll go with you," Robyn said. "I think the rest of you should stay behind. . . just in case."

"I want to go too," Nick protested. "I can help get the boat offshore."

"Well, OK," Johnnie said. "Let's go!"

Robyn ran behind Johnnie's chair and pushed him through the woods back onto the road. "You'll have to push me until we get to the boards," Johnnie told her. "From there I think I can manage."

Nick ran on ahead as the scout. They arrived at the back of the barn and stayed close to the walls. Inside they could hear the muffled sounds of the men as they climbed up the ladder to the hayloft. "Quick!" whispered Johnnie. "It sounds like they're upstairs. Let's get to the path before they come back down."

Pushing with all her might, Robyn maneuvered Johnnie's chair to the plywood path. Once on the boards, Johnnie's strong arms took over. Nick ran alongside him on the sand, and Robyn stayed close behind in case Johnnie's chair slipped. The dune had a steep decline. Fortunately, the wide boards were laid straight. Johnnie took off down the far side of the dune at a frightening speed. Neither Robyn nor Nick could keep up with him. It looked as if he were going to land in the lake, but toward the end of the run, his chair veered off the boards and hit the sand. The impact sent Johnnie flying out of his wheelchair and onto the sandy beach.

Helpless to do anything to stop him, Robyn and Nick ran as fast as they could down the sandy slopes and over to where Johnnie was sprawled. "Are you OK?" Robyn yelled, her face dark with worry.

Johnnie pried his face out of the sand and squinted at his two friends. "Wow!" he said. "That was cool!"

Glancing back toward the lake, Johnnie could see the motorboat beached just a few feet from where he had landed. He rolled over to the boat, grabbed ahold of its side and pulled himself toward the rear. With Nick and Robyn's help, he hoisted himself into the back of the boat. Nick and Robyn pushed with all their strength until the boat was afloat. Quickly they pulled themselves up and over the side. Once they were safely seated, Johnnie gave a tug at the outboard motor's rope. The motor sputtered, then died.

Grasping the handle more firmly, Johnnie tugged with all his might. This time the motor started without hesitation. Pushing the throttle forward slightly, Johnnie eased the boat out toward the center of the lake. Then at full throttle, he began steering the boat around in circles.

"What are you doing?!" Robyn yelled.

"I'm making sure those guys hear us!" Johnnie yelled back over the noise.

After circling a couple of times, Johnnie headed the boat to the opposite side of Gun Lake. Robyn and Nick clung to the sides of the boat as they stared back intently at the sand dune.

***

Travis closed his eyes and held his breath. The creaking of the stall door being opened was abruptly interrupted by the younger man's shouts. "Hey! Al! He's getting away! Come out here! I think he stole our boat!"

Al cursed as he abandoned his search and ran out of the barn. Both men sprinted toward the sand dune just as the motorboat sped away to the opposite shore.

Travis sprang from his hiding place, then stopped. What if the men turned back? Staying in the shadows, Travis made his way toward the open barn doors. His heart pounding, Travis quickly glanced outside. It was all clear. Using every ounce of athletic skill he had, Travis darted out of the barn and sprinted toward the road. Danny called out Travis' name as loudly as he dared to get his attention. Travis saw his friends waving wildly at him and ran full speed to where they were waiting.

Badly shaken and out of breath, Travis felt like he was going to cry. Katy and Joey gave him hugs—they too were on the verge of tears. Danny, his voice shaking with emotion, said, "Come on! We'll have time for a happy reunion later, but we've got to take the shortcut through the woods to the other side of Gun Lake."

"Why?" Travis asked, trying to regain his composure. And then looking around, said, "Where's Robyn, Nick and Johnnie?"

Danny hastily explained the plan. "Hurry!" he said. "We've got to meet them on the other side!"

"Wait a minute!" Travis said. "How did Johnnie get his wheelchair into the boat?"

The four of them looked at each other speechlessly. Finally Travis said, "Look, you guys go on ahead. I'm going over to the top of the dune and find out what's happening."

Before anyone could protest, Travis took off running down the road, past the barn and toward the dune.

***

Down on the beach where their boat had been waiting, Al and his partner were checking out Johnnie's toppled wheelchair. "You mean to tell me," Al snarled, "that the guy who broke into the barn, took one of our CDs and now stole our motorboat is a cripple?!" His face was red with rage.

By the time the two men had reached the shoreline, the motorboat was sending up an impressive spray of water as Johnnie wasted no time getting to his destination.

"Looks like there's more than one person in the boat," the younger man commented.

"Well, if one of them is a cripple, they're not going to get too far too fast without this," Al said as he kicked the wheelchair's tire. He turned to the other man and gave a rough laugh. "Come on, this ought to be a real kick!"

The two men began running along the shoreline toward the place where the motorboat was now docking. The small sandy beach quickly gave way to huge rocks and driftwood, over which the two men had to navigate. Stumbling and cursing, they began narrowing the distance between them and the kids.

***

When Travis reached the top of the dune, he crouched down low in the dune grass. He watched the men scramble over the rocks. In the distance he could see the motorboat— a mere silhouette against the burnt orange sunset. Without wasting a moment, Travis slid down the dune and headed for the wheelchair. Glancing in the direction where the two men were struggling on the rocks, Travis yanked the wheelchair out of the sand, headed for the plywood boards and pushed the chair with all his might up the hill to the top. He stopped only a second to catch his breath. Then, as the night shadows began to swallow up the remaining light, he ran pushing Johnnie's wheelchair toward the path Danny and the others had taken. The thought of what would happen if the men caught up with Johnnie and the others sent a surge of energy through him. Running as if an entire football team were chasing him to the end zone, Travis crashed through the path and nearly ran over Joey, who had stopped in fright at the approaching noise.

***

"They're coming after us!" Robyn shouted. "Quick! Let's get this boat up on the shore."

"No problem!" Johnnie said. "Hang on! And put these seat cushions in front of you." Keeping the throttle open as far as it would go, Johnnie aimed the speeding motorboat toward the shore.

Nick sat like a statue in the boat, his eyes riveted on the fast-approaching beach. His teeth were clenched. A picture of the boat hitting the beach and sailing right up into the woods flashed through his mind. Just when he thought he was going to explode from fright, Johnnie turned off the motor and the boat's forward momentum carried them swiftly but safely onto the beach. Robyn and Joey leaped out. Joey held the boat steady while Robyn helped Johnnie onto the sand.

"What can I do to help you?" Robyn cried out, her face filled with worry.

"Nothing!" Johnnie answered. "I can pull myself up the dune and into the woods. I'll hide there while you and Nick find the others and get help." He could barely see Robyn's face in the dimming light, but he knew she was scared for him. "Hurry!" he said. "I'll be fine! I do this sort of stuff all the time." He laughed lightly, trying to sound reassuring.

Robyn could hear the men's voices in the distance and she knew they would reach them in just a few more minutes. Quickly she grabbed Nick's hand and pulled him toward the woods. Nick was about to protest when Robyn said in a firm but hushed tone, "We've got to get help, Nick! Now!"

In the meantime, Johnnie wasted no time pulling himself up the sloping dune toward the woods. "Gotta get into some dune grass so they won't see my body print," he said as he strained against the cool sand. The broad dune grass cut against his arms and legs as he pulled himself through it and toward the outer edge of the woods. The men's voices were becoming more distinct now. Johnnie was increasingly grateful for the fast-darkening sky.

Once he reached the woods, it was almost too dark for him to see anything. He had to be careful to be as quiet as he could as he steadily pulled himself deeper into the nearby brush. He could dimly see the figure of the first man as he climbed over the last set of rocks. Holding his breath, Johnnie waited.

"Johnnie!" A hushed cry came from the direction of the woods. "Where are you? It's me—Travis!"

Glancing toward the beach where the two men had just arrived, Johnnie was afraid to answer. Frantically thinking what he should do, Johnnie felt around on the ground until his fingers touched something round and hard with a rough "cap" on it. An acorn! He threw the acorn in the direction of Travis' voice. Johnnie heard it plunk against a nearby tree. Soon he could hear scuffling sounds of footsteps getting closer. Gee, Travis was sure making a lot of noise! Johnnie thought. With a watchful eye on the men, Johnnie whispered, "Over here."

Travis headed toward the direction of Johnnie's voice. He was nearly at the edge of the woods and could see the two men standing over by the boat. Johnnie saw Travis as he approached, and he saw the reason why Travis was making so much noise—he was still pushing Johnnie's wheelchair. Wordlessly, Johnnie reached out his arm and touched Travis' leg. He heard Travis gasp in surprise.

"That you, Johnnie?" Travis whispered as quietly as he could, a tremor running through his body.

"Yeah!" Johnnie said. Despite the circumstances, Johnnie had to smile when he realized he had scared Travis out of his wits.

Travis reached down and grabbed Johnnie by the arm. "Get in!" he ordered in hushed tones.

Johnnie reached out and felt the metal frame of his wheelchair. He allowed Travis to help him as he pulled himself into its seat. "OK!" Johnnie whispered when he was securely seated.

The added weight of Johnnie's body and the rough terrain of the woods made pushing the wheelchair difficult. Travis had almost made it to the path, where the others were waiting, when from behind them a gruff voice barked out, "You'd better give it up now, kids. I've got a gun!"

CHAPTER EIGHT

The Chase!

FOR THE FIFTH TIME IN THE LAST HALF HOUR, Mrs. Randall stood on the front porch step and looked intently in the direction of the woods. The quickly darkening sky made it difficult to distinguish shapes. As much as she tried to dismiss the thought, a feeling welled up inside her that told her something was wrong.

As she walked back into the house, Mr. Randall looked up at her from the couch, where he was comfortably propped watching the end of a movie on TV. "They've been this late before," he said. "I'm sure—"

Mrs. Randall looked down at him, her jaw set. "I am sure too," she said quietly. "I am sure they're in trouble. I can't tell you why I feel this way, I just do. I'm calling the other parents."

Mr. Randall knew better than to say anything more. The look on his wife's face told him she was determined. And the thing of it was, when she had these "feelings" about things, she was usually right.

He arose from the couch and took the telephone receiver from her hand. "I'll call," he said. "I'll ask the dads to meet me at the woods, and we'll search together. They're probably just down at the beach. It's lighter there, you know."

Within 15 minutes, a search party was organized. There were several paths along the road that led into the woods. The men agreed to pair off. Travis' and Robyn's fathers took the road that led to the McGruther barn. Nick's and Joey's fathers found a path about 500 feet south of the road. Mr. Jacobson and Mr. Randall drove down about a quarter of a mile until they found another path that would lead them to the far shore of Gun Lake.

There was no moon to guide them, so they had to rely solely on their flashlights. The lake breeze blowing into their faces was cool and refreshing after such a hot and humid day, but the constant roaring of the surf on Lake Michigan made it difficult to hear distant noises. The men estimated the distance from the roadway to Gun Lake was a little less than a quarter of a mile.

As they walked, Mr. Jacobson asked, "What makes you so certain they are in these woods?"

Without looking back, Mr. Randall replied, "Sunsets over the lake can be pretty tempting. Even though it's dark here in the woods, you'd be surprised at how light it still is at the lake. Besides, if they were at someone's house, I'm sure one of them would have phoned."

***

Barely allowing themselves to breathe, Johnnie and Travis remained absolutely still. Danny and the others had heard the man's voice and froze on the pathway. There was no way anyone could talk for fear they'd be heard.

Danny knew that Johnnie and Travis were only 20 or 30 feet from the path. Hearing no sounds, he figured they were hiding in the bushes and hadn't been discovered yet. Judging from where the sound of the man's voice came, Johnnie and Travis' pursuers were not too far behind them.

Danny turned his head and caught a glimpse of Joey and Nick. They were barely visible in the darkness. Carefully and quietly, Danny tiptoed over to where they were standing. He bent down close to Nick's ear and whispered, "I'm going to make some noise to throw those guys the trail. As soon as you hear it, I want you to grab Joey and run back on the path toward the road. Keep running, no matter what, and get help!"

Nick's wide eyes betrayed his fear, but he took a big breath and nodded. Joey, who was standing nearby, didn't know what Danny had said, but he nodded too.

Just then, Danny heard leaves crunching. The men were obviously on the move and from the sounds of it, headed toward the area where Johnnie and Travis were hiding. Frantically, Danny dropped to the ground and began feeling around. He grabbed a handful of acorns and small pebbles and tossed them as hard as he could in an area away from his friends.

"What was that?" a hoarse voice whispered.

"C'mon," said a gruff voice. "It came from over there."

Much to Danny's relief, he heard the footsteps moving off in another direction.

Meanwhile, Travis and Johnnie watched as the faint outlines of the two men moved off away from them. Still, they dared not move. The man who said he had a gun had come so close to the footrest on Johnnie's chair that Johnnie was afraid he would trip over it. A surge of anger and energy had come over him, and he felt like screaming out a fierce battle cry and throwing himself out of the chair in an effort to grab and disarm the man. The feeling was so intense that he had to work hard to stay calm and quiet. Travis must have sensed Johnnie's mood, because just when Johnnie thought he couldn't take another second of all the silence and waiting, Travis put his hand on his shoulder. The unexpected feeling of Travis touching him was enough to calm him.

As soon as Nick heard the acorns hit the ground and the men begin to move toward the sound, he grabbed Joey's arm and swiftly but quietly headed back down the path. Katy and Robyn, who were nearby, saw Danny throw something. Without a word, they picked up on what he was trying to do.

Robyn bent down and found several large stones. Katy found a part of a rotted log. They both edged their way back into the woods off the path. They could hear the men carelessly tramping their way through the underbrush. They were coming closer to where the path was. Suddenly, Robyn hurled one of the larger stones into the woods, trying to make it land in front of the men. Her plan worked. Al yelled out, "OK! I hear you and I'm going to start shooting if you don't stop."

Their footsteps quickened. Katy stepped out onto the path and threw the piece of wood. It landed with a thud a ways behind where the men were headed. Scrambling for more things to throw, Danny joined the girls. They began throwing things in all directions. They could hear the men running, cursing and crashing into things. If they could keep the men distracted and disoriented long enough, Nick and Joey would have a chance to bring help. The question was, could Danny, Robyn and Katy keep from being discovered?

When the commotion started, Travis took his cue and wheeled Johnnie out onto the path. "Go on!" Johnnie urged. "Find the others. I'll be OK."

Travis hesitated a moment, but Johnnie became even more insistent. "I'll be OK—honest!"

Stumbling slightly over some exposed tree roots that were by the side of the path, Travis began running down the path toward all the noise. He stopped a few feet away from Johnnie, turned and said in a loud whisper, "You'd better be!"

Johnnie smiled. It wasn't like he and Travis had become best friends or anything even close to that, but at least Travis had shown some concern. At least he's talking to me! Johnnie thought happily.

In the distance, Johnnie could hear the voices of the men mingled with occasional dull thuds, crackling branches, crunching leaves and the sound of things hitting tree trunks. He didn't hear any kids yelling out so he assumed they were OK. Well, nothing to do but get out of these woods, Johnnie thought as he began slowly pushing the wheels of his chair forward. The path was narrow, but his chair could still fit.

While he struggled to lift his left wheel over a tree root, it occurred to him that the sounds of footsteps were getting closer, as were the men's voices.

Pushing as hard as he could, Johnnie managed to push the wheel over the root. He had to find somewhere to get off the path and hide. Sweaty hands were losing their grip on the handrims. He was alone. Travis had gone on ahead. All the other kids were somewhere on the path. The fear that welled up inside him caused him to panic and feel weak. It was a feeling he had dealt with before—like on his very first day of school, when he had been the first child in a wheelchair to ever go to public school in his hometown.

While most of the kids had been accepting—and curious—the stares from some of the parents and teachers made him feel very uneasy. Being out in the public, away from the protection of his parents and family, was a very scary place to be.

And now here he was somewhere between the far shore of Gun Lake and the barn, in a totally unfamiliar woods, his friends somewhere up ahead and his enemies close by. Someday I'm going to write a book about this, he said to himself. He tried to laugh off the fear he felt but the reality of what was happening was no laughing matter.

Johnnie decided to bulldoze his way through whatever was growing on the right-hand side of the path. Closing his eyes so he wouldn't get poked with branches, he rammed his chair into a small grove of sassafras trees. The slender young tree trunks bent slightly as the oncoming wheelchair pushed forward, but they did not yield.

Suddenly, Johnnie felt his chair jerk backward. With his right hand, he reached over his left shoulder and, with a shudder, felt a hand on the push handle of his chair.

"Thought you were pretty smart, didn't you?" Al snarled.

***

Stumbling, falling and scrambling on shaky legs, Nick and Joey plunged down the path toward the road that would lead them home and to help. They had nearly cleared the woods when Nick stopped dead in his tracks, causing Joey to crash right into him.

"Hey! What's the idea—" Joey began, but Nick interrupted him.

"Shhh! Look!" he whispered, pointing up the path.

Ahead of them the boys could see two small flickers of light.

"It's the other men from the big boat!" Joey almost screamed. The unexpected tears carved little pathways down his hot and dirty face. The events of the night simply became too much for him, and he collapsed in a heap of sobs on the path. Nick was desperately trying to calm him and keep him quiet.

The beams of light pointed in their direction, which only made Joey cry harder. Then some familiar voices called out, "Travis! Robyn! Kids! Is that you?"

Nick recognized Robyn's father's voice. "Yes!" he called out, as tears of relief welled in his eyes. "Yes! We're over here. Hurry!"

Mr. Anderson ran ahead while Travis' father followed. In between sobs and gasps, the two boys explained what was happening. "And they've got guns!" Joey said, starting to cry all over again.

Just then the headlights of a car reflected off the trees, causing the men and boys to turn toward the road. With great relief Mr. Anderson recognized the police cruiser. He waved his flashlight wildly and yelled out. The cruiser stopped and the officer aimed a bright spotlight in their direction. The men helped Nick and Joey to their feet and hurried them over to the cruiser.

"Officer! Are we glad to see you!" Mr. Anderson said.

"Mrs. Randall called saying there were some missing children. She thought they might be in these woods. I see you've found them!" the officer said with a smile.

"No! Well, yes, we found these two. But there are more, and they're in trouble!" Mr. Anderson sputtered. He lost no time in telling the policeman what was happening. Taking one look at Joey and Nick's pale faces and frightened eyes, the officer radioed for help.

***

Travis ran as hard as he could toward all the commotion. A few times he thought he had caught a glimpse of someone running in the woods. The sounds of the men's voices were louder. He slowed to a light jog as he strained to hear the sounds or to see his friends. He had almost come to a complete stop when, out of nowhere, something big and heavy hit him on the side of the head. Dazed, he fell to his knees and then slowly the dark night became total blackness.

***

"I think we hit one of them," Danny said in a low whisper. Exhausted from throwing objects and dashing in and out of the woods, the children crouched down behind some bushes to listen. No longer could they hear any voices, and the constant breeze rustling through the leaves of the trees made it difficult to hear footsteps. It seemed to them they were all alone.

It was the unmistakable crack of a breaking stick that alerted Danny, Katy and Robyn to the fact that someone was very near. Trying hard not to breathe too hard, the three kept very still. The footsteps were only a few feet from them, when suddenly a voice called out, "Hey! Over here. There's a body on the path."

Flickering flashlights were accompanied by the sound of running feet. "Oh no! It's Travis!"

At the mention of Travis' name, Robyn jumped up and ran out of the woods toward the men. Startled, Nick's father shone the flashlight in Robyn's eyes. "Robyn!" he said. "Where are the others?"

"Oh, Mr. Tysman! Am I glad to see you!"

Just then Danny and Katy emerged from their hiding place. With shaky voices, the three children explained what had happened. "We thought the men were in front of us.

Then I saw someone standing on the path just a few feet away from us and I was sure it was one of them. I threw the log as hard as I could. . . " Danny stopped, unable to go on.

Joey's dad put his arm around Danny's trembling shoulders. "I would have done the same thing, if it had been me. You had no way of knowing it was Travis."

Mr. Tysman, who was bent over Travis, said, "I think he's coming around now. Looks like he'll have a nasty bruise on his head, but I think he'll be OK."

Danny, Katy and Robyn rushed over to where Travis was still sprawled out on the path. His eyes were beginning to open and he groaned. Looking up, he saw Danny and the girls. "So there you are!" he said. "Is everybody else OK?"

Before anyone could answer, Mr. Tysman said, "Looks like we have company." Everyone looked down the path. Three sets of flashlight beams illuminated the pathway. "Over here!" Mr. Tysman called out.

Mr. Anderson ran over and gave Robyn a big hug. "Are you OK?" he asked anxiously.

It didn't take Mr. Hughes long to recognize that it was his son who was lying on the ground. He rushed over and knelt down. "What happened? Who hit you? Was it those men?"

Danny slowly moved toward Mr. Hughes. "No sir," he

said, his voice shaking. "I hit him. I-I thought he was one of the men who was chasing us. I'm sorry—I didn't mean. . ." And the rest of his words dissolved into tears.

Mr. Hughes stood up and placed his hands squarely on Danny's shoulders. "Danny," he said sternly. "You did it to protect yourself and the girls. We all know how you feel about Travis. You're all friends. It's going to be OK—and so is Travis." By this time Travis had sat up and thought he was ready to stand.

"I've gotten hit harder than that before in football," Travis groaned as he staggered to his feet. "Now, if you could throw a football like that, I might let you on my team!"

Danny smiled, grateful for Travis' sense of humor. "It was a good throw, wasn't it?"

The police officer instructed Mr. Hughes to accompany Travis and the other children back to the road. "Looks like we have one more to find," he said, his voice grim.

***

Johnnie looked up and saw a menacing face drawing closer to him. Al's breathing came in short, hard bursts and the sweat from his chin dripped onto Johnnie's shoulder. Al moved around to the front of the chair and leaned over, his left hand gripping the wheelchair's armrest and his right hand pointing a gun at Johnnie's face. Johnnie didn't say a word.

"So, thought you'd mess with the big guys!" Al's foul breath almost made Johnnie gag. "Where's the CD you stole, kid?"

Johnnie remained silent. All he could think of was, Here I am—alone. This guy is going to blow me away!

"What's the matter," Al growled. "Are you crippled in your mouth too? Answer me! Where's that CD?"

The familiar feeling of anger and energy began flowing through Johnnie's veins. The urge to rip out the man's lungs flashed through his mind. Unconsciously, Johnnie clenched his fist. His jaw was set and his upper lip curled in a snarl.

Al leaned in even closer. "I'm giving you one last chance, boy!"

This time there was no Travis to offer him a calming hand on the shoulder. This time the urge to yell and scream and lunge was free to take flight. Suddenly, Johnnie could clearly see the man's ugly face. It mocked him. It threatened to undo everything he had ever worked hard to accomplish. At that moment, Al represented every cruel remark Johnnie had ever heard—every disgusted look he had ever endured. He hated that face! And regardless of whether the man had a gun or a flamethrower, Johnnie could not sit in his wheelchair any longer.

From deep inside him came a yell that would have sent chills down the back of a Tyrannosaurus Rex. Using the strength of his upper body, Johnnie gripped the armrests of his chair and propelled himself headfirst into the man's face. The chair jolted backward as Johnnie and the surprised Al crashed onto the ground, with Johnnie landing squarely on Al's chest. At the same moment, the gun fired. Screaming and banging his fists into Al's face, Johnnie hardly heard his father's voice yelling at him.

"Johnnie! Johnnie!" Mr. Jacobson yelled as he frantically ran toward his son. Mr. Randall caught up and helped him pull Johnnie off the man, who was desperately trying to cover his face from the attack.

The gunshot soon brought the other men and police officers. An officer spotted the gun lying on the ground near Al, who was still struggling. In a swift movement, he kicked the gun away while one of the other police officers handcuffed Al and dragged him to his feet.

In the midst of all the confusion and heavy breathing, a low groan could be heard coming just a short distance from where they all were. Two of the officers directed their powerful flashlight beams in the direction of the sound.

There in a crumpled heap lay Al's partner. He was on his side, holding his leg and groaning. "I guess we know where that bullet went," one of the officers commented after examining him. The officer roughly helped him to his feet.

"Let's go," he said, putting an arm around the man's waist to help him walk. "You'll live."

"Come on," Mr. Jacobson said after helping Johnnie back into his wheelchair. "Let's go home."

CHAPTER NINE

What Happened Next!

THANKS TO THE CHILDREN, THE COAST GUARD WAS alerted to the presence of the yacht, which had headed back across the lake after the men failed to reappear. The yacht was stopped. FBI agents searched the barn and found the secret room, just as Johnnie and Travis told them they would. All of the CDs were confiscated.

As it turned out, what Johnnie had stumbled on was part of a huge CD pirating ring. The arrest of the two men and all who were aboard the yacht led to the close of the illegal import business.

Though the kids were local heroes, their parents had a few words to say to them about being included in future adventures.

***

Travis' injury turned out to be minor. He was amazed when the others told him about how Johnnie "was all over that guy," referring to Johnnie's "GI Joe" tactics with Al. Travis just shook his head. He had a lot to think about. Regardless of what he thought Johnnie could or could not do, Travis couldn't imagine any future adventures without his new "friend on wheels."

A portion of the proceeds from sales of *The Barn at Gun Lake* goes to support the nonprofit organization Alternatives in Motion, founded by Johnnie Tuitel in 1995. The mission of Alternatives in Motion is to provide wheelchairs to individuals who do not qualify for other assistance and who could not obtain such equipment without financial aid.

For further information or to make donations, please contact Johnnie Tuitel at:

Alternatives on Motion
1916 Breton Rd. S.E.
Grand Rapids, MI 49506
(616) 493-2620 (voice)
(616) 493-2621 (fax)

Alternatives in Motion is a nonprofit 501(c)(3) organization.